Grow Up, Cupid

GROW UP, CUPID

June Oldham

DELACORTE PRESS/NEW YORK

Published by
Delacorte Press
1 Dag Hammarskjold Plaza
New York, New York 10017

This work was first published in Great Britain by Viking Kestrel.

Manufactured in the United States of America
First U.S.A. printing
Library of Congress Cataloging in Publication Data

Oldham, June.
Grow up, Cupid.
Summary: Baffled by the complexities of love and
tempted to give up men entirely, young Mog starts writing
a romance novel and stumbles upon an unexpected
romance of her own.
I. Title.
PZ7.04539Gr 1987   [Fic]
ISBN 0-385-29544-8
Library of Congress Catalog Card Number: 86-19662

For Abigail, my daughter, who,
reading the first chapter,
laughed in all the right places
and so encouraged me
to continue this book.

Grow Up, Cupid

ONE

The town hall clock whirred dryly, gave an arthritic creak, and began to strike the hour.

Three floors below its grinding mechanism a clerk in the district education office walked to a filing cabinet, opened a drawer labeled "Post O Level on Roll," and flicked through the cards. As with a punitive jab she stamped TRANSFERRED across the name Margaret Dermot, a conversation in a house ten streets away tacked confusedly into its second hour.

"I don't know why you let her done it," Great-aunt Edith said. "In my day, we didn't *want* to leave school. With brains like hers, she could have been a monitress."

"She's going to the Tech, Aunt Edith," Mrs. Dermot stated again.

"That dump! It used to be the workhouse."

"They've done it up since then."

Aunt Edith sniffed. "That's as may be. You always said she was going to school till she was eighteen. Strikes me there's something fishy."

"I don't know why you should think that."

Aunt Edith dipped another biscuit into her tea and sucked the limp end. "I'll tell you why," she answered through the mush. "You can say what you like, but I'm of the opinion that there's a young man in it somewhere."

"Aunt Edith, what an idea! Just because Maggie is finishing off her A levels, it doesn't mean there is any trouble with a young man."

But the suspicion had found a vulnerable spot. Ever since the day Margaret had been observed in the playground lifting her dress and showing her underpants to a circle of uninterested boys, Mrs. Dermot had feared for her daughter's morals. The subsequent twelve years spent in tremulous vigilance had done nothing to relieve her anxiety. Her hand shook as she offered Aunt Edith a plate of lemon curd tarts. Noting this, Aunt Edith took two and sniggered.

The young man in it somewhere was sitting behind his desk staring at an empty tray marked OUT and fingering a pile of unopened correspondence. Though young from the viewpoint of Aunt Edith, Mr. Dab was old enough to have lost, as hostages to the years, much of his cerebral hair and an athletic figure. That is how he referred to what others called bald and fat. The memory of one such description, coupled with the epithet *lazy,* provoked a sudden spasm. Mr. Dab leaned forward, stabbed a nail-bitten finger at his dictating machine, and began to speak.

"To the Director of Education etc. Dear Michael, I find it hard to accept your comments on the transfer of a recent pupil at my school to Nathaniel Chubb. The decision that she should leave this school and complete her studies there was made after a full and frank discussion between me and the girl herself." As he uttered the last words, Mr. Dab's voice was reduced to a croak. Full and frank discussion with Margaret Dermot! A stricken whinny issued from Mr. Dab's throat, entered the dictating machine and later the ear of his startled secretary. A full and frank . . . Mr. Dab's fingers scrambled through the box of chocolate liqueurs camouflaged by the latest *Exchange & Mart*. Miserably he took a nip of the Tia Maria, not one of his favorites, and listened to the feeble strokes of the town's clock. They suggested a knell. But he should be happy. The Mog had gone. And, as she had pointed out, he could quickly grow another spare tire over his conscience. Mr. Dab shuddered.

At that moment Mog was crushed in a lavatory sharing her first cigarette of the day. Smoke writhed upward, took a turn round the abbreviated chain, and formed a swelling mushroom under the chipped cistern. These aesthetic deficiencies suggested that the college was living up to Aunt Edith's opinion.

"It's nice, you coming here. I never thought you and me would be doing this again," Josephine said, inhaling blissfully.

"There's nothing to stop you coming in for a quick drag."

"I wouldn't like to. It would be like secret drinking; worse, somehow, by yourself."

Throughout their years together running the gauntlet of formal education, Josephine's lack of moral fiber had been a frequent sadness to Mog. "All the more reason for doing it," she encouraged.

"Oh, no. I think it's better with somebody." Not wishing to give Mog the opportunity to challenge this concept of vice less vicious if shared, she added hastily, "Anyway, you can smoke in the cafeteria if you want."

"Then why are we in here?" Mog demanded.

As the other took refuge in a bout of coughing, Mog reflected that three terms engaged in shorthand and typing had weakened Josephine's intellectual grasp. It was lucky she was joining her at Nathaniel Chubb.

"Don't let it worry you," she comforted. "As it happens, this is my last, unless anyone likes to offer me one. I need the cash."

Recovered, Josephine asked, "What have you done with the money you earned at the Singing Kettle?"

"Put it under my mattress."

"Sounds uncomfortable."

"It isn't comfort I'm aiming for." Mog drew on the damp butt of the cigarette and flipped it into the toilet. "And there's something else I'm giving up: men."

Josephine coughed again. It was clear that she would derive more than financial benefit from the prohibition on smoking. She had never really got the hang of it, no doubt because, guilty, she had cut down on the necessary practice.

"Giving up men? Do you mean Keith Simpson?" Josephine finally managed.

"He stretches the description—but, yes."

"You'll soon come across another fella," Josephine consoled.

"Come across another? You come across them all the time! You can't miss them: at home, in the library, in shops, on buses. They're everywhere. They flash their teeth at you on TV and boom their voices at you on the radio. In fact, since they comprise half the human race, they're difficult to avoid."

After a year's rest, this exposure to Mog's oratorical gifts, particularly within the confines of a school lavatory, left Josephine shaken. "Well, there you are, then" was all she could say.

"I'm not looking for a replacement, Jo. When I say I'm giving up men I do not refer to a single sample but the whole species. They just aren't worth the bother."

"You used to think they were," the other commented, on surer ground now. "You didn't exactly avoid them. Like that instructor at the swimming baths."

"True," Mog conceded. "You could say that he was one of the chosen, but he didn't appreciate it. It wasn't easy, pretending to be in trouble so that he had an excuse to dive in, but after the sixth dramatic rescue and some strenuous resuscitation, he fell into the habit of disappearing as soon as I turned up. I did succeed in cornering him once and telling him he'd get on better if he gave me the kiss of life, then he changed his shift."

Josephine giggled.

"He was a wet, probably the result of his occupation. Then there was that batch of young masters we got in the freshman year. Their attitude was depressing when you consider that there should be close cooperation between pupils and staff. All I was trying to do was bring them out! And the boys, even juniors, were no better. I should have given them all up years ago. As early as the sophomore year I realized that men, to generalize slightly, are either all pimples or twitch."

"Mr. Dab wasn't. Give him his due."

"That's what I gave him all right."

"And he won."

"A Pyrrhic victory," Mog declared grandly. "All the same, another good reason for my decision."

"You'll get over it," Josephine commiserated.

"I've made up my mind," Mog answered, and flushed the toilet.

"There's nothing against that. You can always change it."

"Not me; I'm not interested," Mog said, watching the cigarette butt swirl around the bowl. "As far as I'm concerned, you can have them. I can see them off as easily as cigarettes."

Ash, tobacco, and water were sucked down the drainpipe as the bowl began to refill. For a moment it was clean, purified of dross. Then the cigarette end, unaffected by its immersion, slid back and danced impudently on the surface. Mog glared.

Having checked on the time for enrollment of new students, Mog left Josephine negotiating her second-year program and walked into the town. She turned into a newsagent's on the main street and began a diligent scan of the magazines, a task she reserved for Thursdays when the latest editions were on display. She had reached the fourth, a thick and expensive affair devoted to photographs of inadequately clad women, when the assistant approached her.

"Can I help you?" he threatened. Dissatisfied with her response, he accused. "You're taking a long time to choose."

"Of course. I don't buy the first one I look at."

"You never buy! You come in here, week after week, have a good look through and walk out!"

"That's because there is never anything worth reading."

"Worth reading! You as good as read the lot. We're not a free library, you know. That magazine is to be bought, and read somewhere else."

"In that case you are selling it on false pretenses. There's nothing to read in it. It's all pictures. Look."

She opened the magazine at the centerfold and held it up. The model, astride a horse, appeared to be imitating Lady Godiva in all details except the hair, which was rather too short to act as the conventional substitute. Observing the assistant's blushes, Mog added, "And you can't even claim that these pictures are exceptionally marvelous. I could show you better than this any day of the week in the showers up at school."

After that she suffered no further interruption.

When she had discovered a magazine offering cash prizes for selected letters and jotted down the address for entries, Mog turned to the free offers. Those available on request she rejected, considering a letter and stamp not worth the result; instead, she found the publications that sought to attract sales by carrying upon their covers a diminutive lure. Generally this would be a lipstick or eyeliner or a small disc of eye shadow, and though these were not always suitable for her coloring, Mog did not hesitate to experiment. Perfection, as illustrated, was dull compared with what improvisation could produce. This week, however, the magazines concentrated on more practical needs. One spawned a tissue impregnated with an astringent alleged to cleanse embarrassing facial pores; another, a puce-colored preparation to cure dandruff; another, a compressed pad with the texture of a loofah to aid monthly confidence. Suffering no embarrassment at the sight of her facial pores, having no dandruff, and already blessed with confidence, Mog declined the gifts. Instead, she removed the pad and arranged it on top of the pile. The assistant's confidence needed a boost. Also, he happened to be an unmitigated nerd. He needed taking in hand.

So did the family security guard, Mog reflected ten minutes later when, walking up the back path to the house, she saw him on duty, his rear end sprawled miserably across the doorstep. At her approach, his haunches twitched in greeting, while in the empty kitchen his throat emitted a plaintive whine. Mog gave his shoulders a tug then, pushing a hand through the cat door, found an ear and pulled. There was a smothered yelp, agitated scrabbling of paws, and the head suddenly popped out. Complete once more, Fred flicked his tail then, puzzled, shadowed it for a couple of wary circles to refresh his memory.

"You and Dad make a good pair," she rebuked him. "When he put that in he never worked out that you would grow too big for it and you still haven't learned that you have. That makes two cases of arrested mental development in the family. No, three," remembering Great-aunt Edith's suggestion that, in that position, the dog could keep an eye on burglars without coming to any harm.

Mog sighed. Sometimes she worried about the quality of her genes.

Apart from Fred, who followed her into the kitchen, attempted to cram himself under a stool, failed, and proceeded to scratch his disheveled scruff, Mog had the house to herself. Though it had been a close shave; traces of biscuit purée and a number of caliper-sized hairpins indicated that Great-aunt

Edith had passed that way. No doubt she had been returned to base before her niece's Thursday afternoon adventure in the supermarket.

Mog sighed again. The energy her mother expended on domestic business would be better rechanneled. Quite into what she could not decide, but she was certain that something should be found to wean Grace from the drug of household and family commitments, some of whose side effects needed careful treatment. On the day that Grace, remarking the brevity of her daughter's underwear, confessed, "I'm not sure if they are decent," Mog could have replied that she had no immediate plans to put their decency to the test, but she refrained; curing someone's delusions at a stroke could be harmful. So she answered, "Don't you worry your little head about them, Mother. It's not underpants boys are interested in nowadays but what's inside them." Wearied after a morning spent loading and unloading the washing machine, Grace was unable to join in the laugh.

Today her mother had satisfied her maternal instincts with a stroke of baking, a heroic achievement in the company of G. A. Edith. Sampling a lemon curd tart and cutting into an egg and bacon flan, Mog suspected that it might be unwise to reform Grace in every particular. But, that worry reserved for later deliberation, she quickly converted the kitchen into an environment suitable for thought: hung her anorak over a cupboard door, flipped her shoes against the radiator, draped her scarf over a burnished plant, left her books on a pile of ironing, wiped the crumbs off her fingers onto a Window Tested tea cloth, fetched the garbage pail, and propped up her feet. Then, relaxed, she considered.

After a time she reached for the pad on which she had noted the details of the magazine competition, found a pen and began, *Dear Ruthy.*

She paused. Ruthy. She picked up her dictionary, a purchase made two years earlier to facilitate verbal exchanges with Mr. Dab. Though of robust construction, frequent use had caused it to deteriorate prematurely. So had Mr. Dab.

"Ruth *(noun, archaic),*" she read. "Pity, compassion." A suitable name for an agony aunt and Mog thought of asking whether it had been chosen for that reason but rejected the query. You did not get three pounds for being clever. In fact, that was half the trouble. The magazine invited letters from readers with "different or original problems." It was not hard to dream up any number of those. The difficulty was to determine the extent of the difference or originality permissible.

At least she could try a new angle.

> *Dear Ruthy,*
>
> *I am a medical student and my girl friend is still at school.* (It struck Mog that in a sentence of thirteen words three inaccuracies were quite an achievement. Keith did not begin his course at Newcastle until October; she had never been, in Ruthy's terms, his girl friend; and if she had been, she certainly was not now. However, this was not the place for subtle qualifications.) *I have always wanted to be a doctor, but she does not seem to share my interest in a properly scientific way. She refuses to help me with simple diagnosis and treatment. For example, when she had strained her left sartorius muscle she utterly rejected my offers, saying that it was not that sort of massage her thigh required. She can be very outspoken. I am not sure whether she is reliable. We cannot get married until I qualify. Do you think in this time she might come around to my way of thinking? I am really worried about this and am exhibiting carbuncular symptoms of stress.*
>
> *Yours anxiously, Keith.*

Mog made herself a beaker of coffee and examined the letter. She decided that the idea had possibilities but needed to be expressed more strongly. Also, it was just possible that a few morons might sympathize. It was necessary to state the other point of view.

Dear Ruthy,

My boyfriend is studying to be a doctor and he says he wants to marry me but we can't until he has qualified. I would not mind that so much if I were sure of his feelings. When we are together he never pays any attention to what I am wearing and he would not notice if I went blond. (I'm a reddish brunette.) All he is interested in is my health. He is forever taking my temperature or listening to my pulse and he asks me the most intimate questions! Sometimes I think he just sees me as a patient, not a normal girl. Are all doctors and doctors-to-be like that? It is another five years before he takes his exams but when I told him that it is a long time to wait, he said I am suffering from a hyperactive libido and he would get a friend to give me a prescription. Do you think I am? I cannot ask any of the girls in my office because they think all medical students are interested in nothing else. I did once. What do you advise?

Worried, Marlene.

That, Mog thought, caught the right tone. She was especially fond of "suffering from a hyperactive libido" but reluctantly altered it to "am oversexed." Not everyone had the *Concise Oxford* handy. Then she made a fair copy. It was, she considered, an interesting example of fiction's debt to life.

Not that Keith had been up to taking her temperature, let alone holding her hand long enough to get the throb of her pulse. Which, to be frank, had never exactly raced in his presence. It puzzled her now why she had ever gone out with him. Discrimination had lapsed. Badly. But that was being too hard on herself, for he had seemed promising at first; no doubt because of those poems he had written to her. Not many guys she knew did that. None, in fact. So that was a definite plus. But he scored nothing for confining his attention to paper. And when her mother would leave her alone in the kitchen with a young man and never mumble a hint that he ought to be going home, no more comment was necessary.

It was a good thing she had discarded men. The amount of effort you could put into them was out of proportion to the results. Not effort, she clarified hastily, such as doing yourself up and making yourself agreeable, but effort of other kinds. For example, in the case of Mr. Dab, trying to overcome his terminal lethargy; in the case of her father, persuading him to see things her way; in the case of Keith, encouraging him to be decisive. She recalled a piece of dialogue with the last:

MOG: What do you want, tea or coffee?
KEITH: I'm easy.
MOG: Well, make up your mind. You're a major.
KEITH: *[Bewildered]* How d'you mean?
MOG: *[Despairing at the stunted vocabulary of scientists]* In other words, you've got the vote! Try exercising it.
KEITH: I don't think tea and coffee are worth voting about.
MOG: But you could practice on them, couldn't you?
KEITH: I don't like arguing with you, Maggie.

Without this unrewarding labor, life was going to be relaxed, serene, equable. Stifling the objection that it might also prove less exciting, Mog opened the prospectus of Nathaniel Chubb and began to skim through.

TWO

"This place has its points," she commented to Josephine next morning. "Since I'm only expected to come in for classes, doing three A levels works out as fifteen hours a week. Add homework, and the total is still less than the time spent in school, seven hours a day, five days a week. We could have cut the working week in the senior year by half if they hadn't insisted on all the unnecessary extras such as assemblies, games, career seminars, moral guidance, health lectures, life skills—that trash. It was all talk and no action, but Dab wouldn't listen, though I explained it to him at some length."

"I bet you did," Josephine said feelingly. "It looks as if you'll have some free time to inspect the talent. You should find something to go at."

Inspection of the talent lined up in the cafeteria that morning revealed that what there was to go at was committed to an alternative activity: twenty or so young men fiercely consuming sausages and chips. Having pushed four tables together, they formed an insular group, thus avoiding the risk of softer temptation while satisfying immediate priorities.

"They're apprentices," Josephine identified. "But they come in only one day a week."

Sometimes Mog worried about Josephine. She told her so.

"I worry about myself. It's months since I got a steady bloke. I could just do with one at the moment. Brightens you up. I'm sick of TV. It's a problem, isn't it?"

"Your problem, not mine," Mog reminded her. "There are alternative forms of recreation."

"Such as?"

The question gave Mog pause. "I'm still working on it. I'll let you know."

The other laughed. "You needn't worry."

Mog thought this a convenient moment to encourage a vigorous reappraisal. Josephine was too young to have settled into a rut.

"Have you ever examined this habit of going out with men, Jo? Or worked out systematically their pros and cons?"

"I can't say that I have. I'm just interested in what things they have going for them."

"You couldn't give me six."

Josephine said decisively, "They're nice to be with."

"In what way? They're a conversational free zone. Look at Keith—three sentences and he's worn out."

"They aren't all like that!" the other claimed with spirit. "And Robin could be funny. I know you didn't like his Benny Hill take-off, but that's just a question of personal taste."

"You're not getting very far."

"All right. They're protective and strong and they like to pay."

This was more than Mog had bargained for. Ignoring the protective bit since her father had that tendency, she wondered at the popularity of body-building gadgets in the light of men's alleged strength and suggested that by paying for the evening a man kept his eye on the main chance.

"A lot of them make good fathers," Josephine argued, a disconcerting wistfulness entering her face.

"They have no competition! How many women do you know who could make a good father?"

That improved Josephine's expression, but she concluded stubbornly, "Well, I think they're sweet."

There are many ways of wasting time, Mog reflected, but she made a final effort. Pretending nonchalance, she said, "You can't be referring to their disposition, so I take it you mean their smell. Frankly, I find the sickly deodorants they spray over themselves nauseating. I'd rather have good honest sweat. But I do draw the line at their farts."

"I've never been out with one that did," Josephine said, leaning forward, eager for details.

Mog regretted that she could not supply any. "Neither have I; but you should hear our Ben."

"That doesn't count! He's only thirteen! He's not a man yet."

"In that case, I hope I'm not around when he is. By the time he's twenty, he'll need a silencer fitted."

At which they were both convulsed.

"Strikes me you've got a bigger problem than I have," Josephine commented. "At least when I've finished homework I know what I'd *like*. That reminds me. I bumped into Keith yesterday. He starts at Newcastle in two weeks. We had quite a chat. Honestly, I don't think he's bad; not bad at all."

"You're right. He hasn't a hint of mischief, vice, sin, dissipation, dissoluteness, libertinage, lasciviousness, licentiousness, lewdness, or—not to put too fine a point on it—lust."

The last word was a help. Josephine thought about it. "I suppose that's a consideration," she admitted, looking blank. "But if that's all you had against him, you'll soon make up. There's the bell; time for me shorthand. Look, if you've nothing to do, you can borrow this. It's our Glenda's library book. At the rate you read you will be half through it by the time you see Mr. Beadle."

She put the book on the table in front of Mog. Together they winced at the cover. As if she were handing out medicine, Josephine persuaded, "It's maybe worth giving it a chance. It might cheer you up."

No matter what arguments she is given, Josephine is convinced that my disaffection with men is caused by falling out with Keith, Mog grumbled to herself. Whereas it was impossible to fall out with him; he refused to indulge in a good ding-dong on the grounds that it meant you did not *care*. That was part of his trouble, not all of it, but a good chunk: he wanted her to be attached. Attachment of an amorous nature she might have been happy to consider, though she had told him that he would have to experiment with means other than his poetry to produce the right vibes; but attachment that required promises, conditions, and the accumulation of hardware was not to be contemplated. "I'm only seventeen," she had reminded him. "Juliet was only fourteen," he had answered. She could see he was pleased with the literary allusion; they didn't come easily to Keith. "And look how that turned out," she had said. After that he had taken the huff, the nearest he had come to a show of temper, and had made no reply when, to prime the flow, she had asked, "Have you ever thought of having a go at blank verse?"

Having a go at any kind of verse might have improved the heroine of our Glenda's library book. "It was not the town she was traveling to with the small amount of money she had carefully saved working in the Remmington Organization but what Dona had left behind her that caused the tears to drip unstemmed down her wan cheeks. It held memories of a dear aunt who had brought her up and given her the love and care that Dona's parents, killed tragically together in a road accident when she was only three years old, had been unable to give. Recalling, Dona felt in her handbag and took out her powder compact. The tears had made such a mess of her face."

In spite of this, Mog persisted and was making good progress when a voice asked, "Fancy a cigarette?"

"Yes." She looked up. "But I've stopped smoking."

"That's convenient," the young man answered, "because I've run out."

Mog kept her face expressionless. "I'm reading."

"I'd never have guessed. A pity about that. You might be interrupted." He bent forward, flipped up the book, and read the title. "Any good? I wouldn't object to a bit of that myself. Trouble is, at the moment there isn't much interest."

He nodded toward the other occupants of the cafeteria. Apart from one decorating the notices on the board with graffiti, most of the remainder were conserving their energies for the second lecture and were hunched in attitudes of meditation over ketchup-smeared plates. On the perimeter was a man in dungarees studying the *Sun* behind which he removed a hip flask and topped up the college tea.

"He's the caretaker, Hard Man Sugden, to be handled with care. Anticipating your remark that you would not wish to handle him with anything, I think you should know that is not the universal opinion; not quite, anyway. The minority view is represented by Noreen the other side of the counter, the one kneading the pig swill."

"Thanks. I was dying to know that." She returned to the book.

"I don't like to introduce a note of criticism into the early stage of a promising relationship, but you can be affected by too much reading; you can lose touch with the real thing."

He paused. "You've just passed up the chance to quip briskly, 'I suppose you think you can supply it.' Don't fret. It may come again. Because I drop in from time to time, keep an eye on this august institution. It's an unsung task, but as a former student—of outstanding merit, of course—I do feel a certain . . . duty."

Usually Mog had no difficulty in cutting out unsolicited distraction, but the television, Aunt Edith's prattle, or Ben's digestive system had been no preparation for this. She turned a page. Perhaps the book was at fault.

"Another danger," he continued, "is too much specialization. Hoping that you are about to deny that you devote every hour God sends to reading paperback romances, I agree with what you are eager to admit: that you can grow narrow, concentrating on one thing. I'm thinking of diversifying as well. For example, I tried for a job yesterday, but I did not get it. We were not compatible."

Mog allowed herself to lift her eyes.

"They gave the impression that they were nervous about their public image. I was wondering whether they could have been influenced by my appearance."

First making a labored search through her bag for a scrap of paper, smoothing out the wrinkles and laying it in the place she had reached, Mog closed the book and scrutinized him. A full minute is a long time to sit opposite a young man and examine his features, but Mog hung on. She added to the suspense by getting up and doing a slow circuit to check on the back view.

"It's possible," she judged.

His hair, in gradations of brilliant color, took its inspiration from tropical plumage, though this effect was somewhat marred by the overall arrangement of gummed spikes. There was also a quantity of earrings, most of them nesting in one lobe.

"In fact, I think you might have overdone it."

He was smiling, relaxed, the epitome of the laid-back, cool, together, infuriatingly unruffable male.

"To every man his excess," he answered.

Why stop at one? Most men can manage dozens without undue fatigue, Mog said to herself as, the fabric of the school vibrating under a peal of electric bells, she made for Mr. Beadle's office. Not that she had any moral objection to excesses; they could introduce some color into the universal drab, like G. A. Edith's obsession with teeth. A good reason for developing a few herself.

It was a pity she had not the odd excess ready for Mr. Beadle, she mourned as she knocked on his door. But you never knew; something might turn up.

"Come!" Mr. Beadle sang out. "Welcome to Nathaniel Chubb! Margaret Dermot, isn't it? I always try to see as many new students as I can fit in, and your name came up." He removed his watch and, affecting carelessness, placed it within glancing distance on his desk. "Please sit. I like to think that I know all my students and that they feel they can come to me at any time, whatever the reason."

Assuming some response was required, but having nothing to go on, Mog asked, "What sort of reason had you in mind?"

Mr. Beadle smiled. "That is for you to choose, Margaret, not for me to impose. Indeed, I think you will find that there is very little imposition of any kind here. I don't know whether you have caught up with Education . . ."

"I've been at school since I was five, so I've picked up quite a bit," Mog pointed out.

"Ah, I mean the Philosophy, the Systems, the new Changing Face."

Not having made the acquaintance of the last, Mog had to take it on trust. Certainly the face opposite her, unlined, trim, with the blush of jogging on its cheeks, was different from the one she was used to. With a flick of nostalgia she recalled the agitated folds of Mr. Dab's capacious flesh.

"And that is what Nathaniel Chubb is all about," the other was saying. "I know that its popular name remains the 'Tech' and though I regret the persistence of that title I do not regret its origin, for that is an unpretentious, no-nonsense base for what we are, or what we shall very soon be: a community college that enters the life of every individual in its catchment, which both leads and serves, which engages the skills of the academic and the craftsman, the technician and the poet, which offers courses tailored to all levels of talent and aspiration from the personnel manager to the modest housewife, a community college that is both a place of recreation and a center of learning in the true sense of the word."

Breathless, he halted. There were several expressions Mog would have liked to comment upon and she would also have liked to question him on how he saw certain members of the community fitting in, but a man of such wild ambition, in this town, deserved encouragement. So she said, "I might be able to get one or two people interested."

Mr. Beadle threw out an arm in a gesture that was hard to interpret. Then he resumed, "And one principle without which this school would founder, without which it would be as a hapless vessel adrift without a rudder, is that *no one is turned away*. For example, despite the great inconvenience to staff involved, I have only this session admitted a young girl who, halfway through her A level courses, wishes to complete them here in one year. As you will appreciate, she will have covered some aspects as yet untouched by the classes she joins and vice versa, yet however difficult this will be for all concerned, I decided that she must not be refused."

"Thanks."

Still at full throttle, Mr. Beadle continued, "And I have not even sought the reason why she left school!"

For a second the triumph of rectitude over curiosity polished his face, then it paled as he assimilated Mog's word. He swallowed noisily.

To help him out, Mog said, "I don't mind giving you the reason: sloth."

The other improvised a laugh. "I can hardly believe that.

Your O level results, if I remember correctly, Margaret, were extremely respectable. More than respectable; almost distinguished."

Mog inclined her head graciously, but his fulsome compensation for his blunder was inducing a recovery that was premature.

"I was not referring to myself, but to Mr. Dab."

Mr. Beadle started and glanced nervously over his shoulder. Then his eyes scurried round the room, appealing for guidance. Finding only a builder's design for additional parking space and a collage of uncensored holiday snaps put together by one of his modest housewives, he ran his tongue over his lips and croaked, "I think it would be best if we agreed that I had not heard that, Margaret. It would be dishonorable of me to be known to permit a student's comment on another member of my profession."

Mog took his point and she liked the way he expressed it. Others might have referred to a Mafia protection racket or a closed shop, but she could see that Mr. Beadle was a man of delicate sensibilities. It was necessary to ignore them, however, in the interest of truth.

"It was not only that he suffered from a basic obese inertia," she confided. "To be honest, Mr. Dab and I just did not get on. I don't know the best way to explain it." But as she spoke, a method occurred to her. Mog leaned back, closed her eyes, and held forth.

"It was something like this:

". . . From the first moment she met him, she had felt this strange antipathy. It was there in the very marrow of her bones and she felt it again as she watched the cynical line of his full lips, saw the mocking expression in his cool, assessing eyes as they followed her beautifully shaped body, the tan of the long hot summer contrasting against the crisp white broderie anglaise blouse which, cut deep, showed off to perfection the rounded firmness of her breasts. She knew this man was dangerous; he threatened her individuality, her hard-won independence, and in his presence she felt on trial, defensive, and often, to her secret horror, defenseless. All this rushed through her mind as his hand came down roughly on her shoulder. For a moment a shudder, as of an electric current, ran through her. Then, with a desperate little cry, almost a moan, she stepped back and pulled herself away . . ."

When Mog opened her eyes she discovered Mr. Beadle in a state of trance. His mouth hung slack and his hands were clenched over the edge of his desk. Such appreciation was pleasing.

He unhooked his fingers and loosened his tie and top button. Fighting for air, he whispered, "I can't believe it. He's a respectable . . ."

Obviously Mr. Beadle had a literal approach to fiction. Overcoming the temptation not to enlighten him, Mog said, "That situation never occurred. I just wanted you to get the general idea of conflict, hostility, that sort of thing."

The other thought about that for some time. Then he ventured, "Did you make it up?"

"I did it extempore. Based on something I've just read."

"Really?" He stroked the papers on his desk. He appeared to be as a vessel adrift. "Is it one of your interests, a hobby?"

"Oh, no. Not at the moment, anyway. I've given up men."

The papers under his hand fanned out and proved difficult to restack. Fumbling, he stammered, "What I meant was, do you write?"

"Only letters to magazines or entering competitions. It's easy to pick up a few pounds that way if you're short."

Mog detected a lack of enthusiasm in Mr. Beadle's stare.

Either he never needed pin (or perhaps, in his case, beer) money, or after that inspired paragraph he had expected higher achievements than a few paltry letters. "Do you advise me to try something longer? Something on the lines of what I've just done?"

He raised his head. Glazed eyes slid across her face. Again he ran his tongue over his lips but exhaustion hindered the words of encouragement.

> . . . It showed in every line of his body as he came round the desk to open the door . . .

Mog stood up.

Seeing this, Mr. Beadle began to revive. With a relief that made him hearty he discovered his place in the standard text. "Well, I'm pleased to have made your acquaintance, Margaret, and hope that you will take advantage to the full of all that our school has to offer. And remember that, as Principal—for my sins—I am here to be consulted at any time, whatever the reason. May I wish you a happy and successful year?"

On the last words Mr. Beadle raised a hand, intending to administer an avuncular pat to Mog's shoulder, but a memory intervened. The hand stopped, flapped around in the air, and then was returned to Mr. Beadle's side. The Principal of Nathaniel Chubb had just learned to insure against risks.

Outside his office Mog hesitated. It was three o'clock and there was nothing on her timetable. The hours were her own to be used as she wished. She ran through a few alternatives: work in the library, a cup of tea in the cafeteria, another letter to the compassionate Ruth. None of these was attractive. She assumed that she must be depressed. This was a condition that required methodical diagnosis.

"First," she began as she walked down the corridor, "I could be suffering from school deficiency, in the circumstances a laughable idea but you can become institutionalized however hard you resist. And it had a few things in its favor, such as skirmishes with the screws and loafing with the old lags. That is not over; I shall see them," she reminded herself. "Except for the redundant Keith, most of them are around."

However, they were not around at that moment; there was a distinct lack of familiar faces as she strode toward the main door.

"Second," she continued, going down the steps and into the street, "I could have given up too many things together: cigarettes and school and men. (In the last group, until I have refined definition, I have to include the pimply Keith. Not that he had any pimples on the bits I could see of him but it is a mistake to generalize from the limited area that men, for most purposes, choose to expose.) To have thrown them all out in one go was probably too drastic. It might have been better to stagger them: school in July, cigarettes in August, and men in September. I must be experiencing symptoms of treble withdrawal. The cure has to be replacement. There are the courses at the school, but I reckon I still need to find other things to take up the slack," she advised herself, crossing a bridge and turning onto a path.

"Third possibility is that I am losing my grip. Here I am, just starting a new place and instead of being euphoric I feel stale. I'm seventeen, once sound of mind and body, and already pitching into senility. In another two and a half years I shall be twenty." She jabbed at a nettle. "At this rate, I might as well give up.

"On the other hand, as G. Aunt Edith says, 'If you're a bit off-color it's likely a touch of the worms.' "

Mog stepped over a trip wire of briers, maimed an elder, trampled over gypsywort, and contemplated the water at her side.

. . . It was a tiny dell surrounded by trees, gnarled and ancient, where flowers of many lovely colors bloomed in profusion and their scents wafted and mingled as if all the stoppers in an exotic perfumery had been removed at once. In the center of this lonely but beautiful spot was a miniature pool set like an exquisite glittering jewel in the velvet grass. Watching the gentle ripples, Dona felt her miseries drop like a heavy weight from her shoulders and she forgot the time Mr. Remmington had ordered her back to her typewriter. What, she wondered, had been the meaning of his hooded look when he came upon her by the swimming pool, clad in her Lycra bikini with the elastic straps? . . .

Further along the towpath there was a man fishing. Considering the color of the water in this stretch of the canal and the weeds fighting for room on its bed, Mog thought his optimism excessive.

It was also excessive in another direction because as she reached him he looked round and asked, "Like me to walk you along?"

"No," she answered.

You would have thought it was impossible to misinterpret that, but few men understand a refusal. Instead, he inquired what she was doing that evening.

It was one of Mog's rules in life never to dismiss a question; it showed a curiosity that was healthy and so obliged a more than casual answer.

She attempted this, described in full her customary pursuits, elaborated those which she thought might interest him most, then went on to explain her difficulty in selection by treating him to a close analysis of her present mood.

This seemed to be infectious because when she had finished

she noticed that he was poking at the maggots in his tin and looking glum.

It was really stupid, Mog thought, the pair of them feeling so miserable. The day was quite reasonable: it had not rained yet; the smell from the gasworks had an unusually mellow flavor; the scum on the surface of the canal looked uncommonly fresh; and the derelict warehouses opposite had a less deserted appearance now that the vandals had moved in.

Some definite action was needed. And as she thought this, Mog

. . . remembered the meeting with the Principal of The Remmington Community College and she found herself going over what he had said, rehearsing his gestures and listening to the subtle innuendoes of every word that to most people would have been commonplace but, with the infallible instinct of a woman, she knew had been special, meant only for her. A shiver passed through her slight but exquisitely formed body, clad only in the pretty cotton dress, freshly laundered, that she had put on that morning. It was frightening, unexpected, but she knew at that moment that an idea, like a child, had been born . . .

"I know what I'm going to do this evening," Mog told the fisherman. "I'm going home and I'm going to start writing something, a story or maybe a book. I've never tried that before and it would be something to do. I need an interesting occupation; I feel useless without. Do you know, it would not have occurred to me to do it if I had not talked to Mr. Beadle up at the Tech." She explained the incident, lingering over the paragraph that had so impressed Mr. Beadle and wondering which sentences he had enjoyed most.

The man made no comment. Mog looked at her watch. She

had given him ten minutes and all he could do was fiddle with his rod.

"I reckon the bit Mr. Beadle really liked," she said, bending over, her mouth close to the man's ear, "was the description of her body tanned by the long hot summer and the way her blouse showed off the shape of her breasts."

The man jerked away. For a moment one foot was lapped by the cooling waters of the canal, then he was scrambling up. "Why don't you lay off?" he demanded.

As Mog left him, she looked back. He was on his knees, rounding up the wriggling maggots that had been knocked from the tin.

THREE

Mog put down her pen and looked around the kitchen. She was feeling hungry. It was remarkable how two hours' thought gave you an appetite, and all she had done was map out a few ideas; she had made no decisions on characters. The chief trouble was to find a man who would fit the requirements. That is, of the books she had been reading during the last fortnight. She had practically stripped the paperback stand in the library, an impossibility in the time she had allowed herself had she not taken the precaution of obtaining tickets for the rest of the family. "Don't you think your dad would be happier with a thriller?" the librarian had inquired, smirking. "No, he has decided he went wrong somewhere and is trying to get a few hints. I'm sure you'll know the feeling," she had answered. As a result he had made a botched job with his stamp. Underweight and cultivating a straggly beard to offset an extending forehead, he was obviously a failed candidate for principal man.

She wondered how other authors went about finding their characters. So far she had never met any men like these, which perhaps was not surprising in this town but you would think that, statistically, it would throw up one or two. Once over that hurdle, she thought there would be no difficulty in writing the book. It seemed an easy way to make money. Returning to her notes, she read through the list of definite purchases—record player, desk for her bedroom, typewriter, replacement for the *Concise Oxford*—and added, small car. You had to be practical. Kept outside their house, anything bigger than a Renault would block up the street. The next pages were headed "Possible Men"; five pages to Mr. Dab, seven to Keith, half a page to her father. She wrote "Mr. Beadle" and after a moment's thought listed: healthy, straight nose, brown eyes, full head of hair, probably decently built but have not seen him in trunks, interested in his job, very appreciative of literature, possibly an outdoor man because not comfortable in collar and tie (see how he unfastens them when distracted), tendency to fiddle with objects on his desk, shows reluctance for physical contact. Caution: He could be a nerd. A more detailed account withheld until our acquaintance has ripened.

Meanwhile, as Aunt Edith would say before she tackled a plate of rissoles and chips, a little light snack would not come amiss. Glancing at the pans burnished with Brillo pads and ready for service in soft female hands, Mog decided on a snack of such proportions in the school cafeteria. Then, with brain reactivated, not a publicized virtue of school nosh, she would review her research and concentrate on plot.

That was not something Keith had to worry about, she reflected when she discovered an envelope from him lying on the front mat. In it was a poem. At present, rather out of season, he seemed to be obsessed by moonlight on unsullied snow. Mog sighed. It was a pity she had not decided to write this book earlier; she could have left the fancy bits to Keith. He also claimed to recollect their voices mingling. This, Mog considered, was taking poetic license too far. Once, after an evening's attempt to improve, by brilliant example, his feeble grasp of conversation, she had accused: "You don't say much, do you?" His response that in her presence speech was unnec-

essary had caused her to wonder fleetingly whether he was
making a joke but humor was a serious matter for Keith and
not to be attempted lightly. Nor, indeed, was anything else, so
Mog was intrigued by the last line: "Eternally in my voluptuous thoughts." Had he got the adjective wrong and really
meant to say "voluminous," or was it carefully chosen? If the
latter, it might indicate that Keith had taken a turn for the
better. And just as he was about to disappear with his Gray's
Anatomy into the dissecting laboratories of Newcastle! On the
other hand, she reminded herself, it is only his *thoughts* that
are voluptuous. Thoughts and words might make a pretty
poem, she told him, filing it among the litter in her haversack,
but he would have employed his time better concentrating on
deeds.

An opportunity to concentrate on some herself was offered
as she entered the school.

"Do you happen to know the times of the buses from the
top?" a woman, much flustered, demanded. "I expected to be
out earlier than this," tugging at the door marked PUSH. "I
have to collect the baby. My friend can only see to her till half
past. I don't like to put her out but she said I'd got to come
because I'd been promising myself I'd start studying as soon as
I'd got the children off my hands and then, just as I did, I fell
for another. It's a problem, isn't it?"

Mog agreed, wondering to which problem the woman referred. But she decided against suggesting a revision course in
contraception and asked why the woman did not put the child
in a day nursery.

There weren't any.

"In that case, there ought to be one here. You would expect
it would be the first thing Mr. Beadle would think of. There
must be hundreds of women—well, dozens—who would do a
course if they had a handy place to stick the kid. A day nursery is a basic facility. Why don't you tell him?"

The other showed no eagerness to do this, arguing nervously that Mr. Beadle had plenty of more important things on his mind.

Mog stared at her. Sometimes she despaired of her sex. It was attitudes like this that kept women where men thought they belonged: at the sink, up to the armpits in suds.

"I don't like being a trouble," the woman explained.

"I do," Mog answered, brightening.

But before she was, food was essential, she decided, and entering the cafeteria, joined those waiting at the counter; it would be unwise to meet Mr. Beadle after a three-hour fast (observing that Noreen still riddled the pig swill) although she did not anticipate he would offer much resistance (taking care to choose a salad with an unpunctured membrane of plastic wrap); not like Mr. Dab. It was amazing the energy that man would expend on avoiding work. Such as tutoring seniors to take his lessons.

"I explained to him that in the hours spent instructing them he could have taught the lessons himself," she told Josephine, having sketched in the episode as she unloaded her tray. "This anyone's seat?"

"Be my guest," Josephine answered after Mog had sat down. "Why were you going into that, anyway? You didn't take German."

"Pupils' representative."

"What?"

"After your time."

"I'm sorry I missed that."

"Dab was sorry he didn't."

Josephine nodded. "He'll be enjoying the rest."

"He enjoyed nothing else! It's a shame he is not seventy-five pounds lighter; he could have been suitable as the fellow in one of your Glenda's library books."

"You're joking."

"I only say that because he would be easy for the heroine to hate. Unfortunately, she has to go for him at the end, and anyway you know from the start that she will do. Come to think of it, the plots never surprise you."

"You are doing. You been reading some more?"

"Dozens, or it feels like it. Look, Jo, I've been meaning to ask you all week. Have you ever met a man six feet three in his socks with a splendidly sculptured head plus raven-black or perhaps sun-bleached curls, with piercing blue or perhaps fathomless brown eyes, with lips whose sardonic curl betrays a sensuous fullness, with virile but sensitive hands professionally manicured without a hint of effeminacy, who despite the fact that he is pushing thirty or even forty has a supple body bearing not an ounce of extra flesh and molded with hard muscle under a golden tan that covers the whole of his frame except perhaps under his bathing trunks where a few inches remain, as yet unrevealed?"

It was a long sentence but Josephine had no difficulty keeping up with it. "Well, now you ask, no." She grinned. "Not in every respect, anyway."

"That's why I cheated and put in the untanned bit under the trunks." At which they both sniggered.

"In addition," Mog continued, "I'd like to know if such a man, with or without the pink strip, has ever with one long step circled your slender body in his arms,

". . . grasped the protesting hands and locked them in one unrelenting fist, brought his head down to the moist lips that were no longer turned away from him and moaning with a passion he could not control, did with teeth and tongue what words could never say, and knowing then his answer, began slowly, teasingly, to unhook the tiny pearl buttons at the shoulder of the Pierre Cardin gown, his expensive and beautiful gift . . .'"

"Oh, stop it, Mog," the other begged. "You're turning me on."

Mog looked at her astonished. There were moments when, in spite of evidence to the contrary, she doubted Josephine's intelligence and sense. There were also moments in her life, albeit few in number, when she could think of nothing adequate to say. This was one of them.

In this slack period Josephine took the opportunity to remark that the piece was not at all bad and that Mog ought to have a go at writing a romance herself. Mog indicated that was her intention. Growing enthusiastic, Josephine suggested some titles: *Body Heat, Torrid Love.* Mog pursed her lips; from hearing that paragraph, Jo appeared to have contracted a fever. Digressing into textual analysis, Josephine commented that if the man had her hands in one of his and his other was unbuttoning her dress, they were in a very ungainly position, but that was a niggling criticism and not one she could endorse from experience. Mog dismissed it with a weary gesture. Taking up the problem of the appearance of the hero, she was able to offer constructive advice: there were several like that in films, though of course they were not men exactly but actors, and the thing to do was fix on some bread-and-butter guy and then add the jam. Mog picked her scalp. Josephine concluded that, unless she was misreading the signs, Mog was interested in men again, a fact she was pleased to note.

"Well, don't bother; I'm not." Mog at last found words.

"Then I don't know how you can write much more of that sort of thing. I reckon you would have to fancy a man."

"I'll manage."

"It would be more fun if you couldn't." Her eyes glinted. "I mean—that bit you've just quoted. Think what it would be like, trying it out!"

"I'm not likely to have a chance. All these blokes are fabulously rich and are either boss man of an international business empire, or an expert in scuba-diving, or the owner of a fleet of luxury cruisers, or a big shot in the college of surgeons. They aren't the sort of fellas you see hanging round the Job Center. But if there were a need for any testing I should approach it in the spirit of scientific inquiry."

Josephine giggled. "That's one word for it."

"I should be perfectly objective." But the other's laughter was infectious. "And if not, we would have to rate it as a sacrifice in the cause of Art."

"Say no more," Josephine implored, the table rocking between them. "Or we'll both get the stitch."

One way or another, this conversation with Jo has given me a lot to think about, Mog said to herself as they parted. But first she must see Mr. Beadle. According to a notice, handwritten to simulate informality, he invited students to make comments and suggestions, thereby insuring their individual contribution to the ethos of the school, which, as their Principal, he welcomed at all times.

This eagerness was not shared by his secretary who, leaping from her cubby, intercepted Mog's knock.

"There is a box for suggestions," she threatened. "Mr. Beadle must not be interrupted by every minute detail of admin. But since you are here, you can tell me. I'm his nuts-and-bolts woman."

Contemplating her appearance, Mog thought the image apt but still unfortunate. "I'd rather tell him; and it's not a minute detail. It is fundamental to the whole organization of the school." For a spontaneous argument, Mog thought that rather good.

Mr. Beadle's secretary was not sympathetic. Her nostrils flexed, disturbing her spectacles. "I suppose you think you can do better than me," she began, but they had been overheard.

"Send her in, Myrtle; I have a teeny minute," Mr. Beadle lilted, and at her master's command Myrtle stepped back.

"Well, what can I do for you?" Mr. Beadle asked, smiling before he recognized her face. "Let me see; you are Mr. Dab's ex-pupil, aren't you? Miss . . . er . . ."

"Margaret Dermot."

"Of course," he agreed warily. "I hope it is not a complaint about lunches. I'm afraid that Noreen has a lot on her hands at the moment."

"I've noticed that," Mog said. Then she explained her mission.

Mr. Beadle was not enthusiastic. "I do not think there would be a use for a day nursery. I have to tell you that there has never been an appeal for one to date."

"That may be that there are not many women here with small children. Because there isn't a nursery. If there were one, they would join classes, but since there isn't, they can't come, so you have never been approached to . . ." She stopped, having worked out that Mr. Beadle was waving a limp hand not to swat flies but to indicate understanding. Just to make sure, she added, "It's a vicious circle."

"I think we are moving into very deep waters, Margaret," breathing strenuously in preparation for the plunge. "There is a strong body of opinion, backed up by clinical observation, that small children need the security of a mother's presence which they can call upon, at any time."

"Half of them don't get it, do they? They're pushed out on the street to play while their mother puts her feet up and has a cigarette."

The other blenched. "I am not sure that I would wish to be held responsible for encouraging women to evade their family responsibilities and leave their young ones to come here."

"They wouldn't be leaving them if they brought them to be looked after. Look, how can you call this place a community college if half the population can't use it? If you had a nursery, you would have mothers here during the day and children as

well. Then it would be a community college in the true sense
of the word."

There was a silence during which Mog detected, to cull a
phrase, a struggle taking place in the Principal's breast. He
coughed painfully.

"It would not demand much organization," she urged, remembering Myrtle. "You only need a room and a few toys.
People would give those. Supervision could be on a rota system. It's simple—nothing to it."

Still he did not speak. And she had even considered him as
model for chief man!

"I suppose most schools like this have a day nursery and it
would be a shame if Nathaniel Chubb was the only one without. If you think about it, there are lots of ways it could be
developed so that it was a valuable part of the curriculum. For
example, you could have the children as casualties—I mean,
specimens—for the nursery nursing classes and the cookery lot
could experiment with suitable menus and some people could
teach the older ones to read and you could introduce them into
seminars on family management. With a bit of imagination
there is no end to what could be done with a nursery. It's just
the sort of thing to put the school on the map."

She paused. Mr. Beadle was signaling a desire to say a few
words himself. They were: "I'll look into it, Margaret." He
appeared incapable of any more.

"That's terrific," she said. "I'll tell the woman she can bring
her baby, then."

Mr. Beadle shuddered. Then he finally capitulated. Having
done so, he became, as Glenda's library books would have it, a
changed man. "Very well, but not before next Monday. There
is much to be done, notices to get out, a small statement to the
press." He leaned forward, his face glowing. "I am pleased
that you brought this to my attention, Margaret. I had not
suspected that without a day nursery the reputation of this

school might be at stake. Nor had I envisaged its potential for establishing Nathaniel Chubb as a school receptive to new ideas, a school in the van of progress, a community college which is a dynamic force in the lives of every member of its catchment and perhaps—who knows?—beyond."

It occurred to Mog that she might have overdone it.

"Well, Margaret, I do not think we should delay our work any longer. Enrollment for evening classes begins this week, which is always a busy time and, for me, one of experiment. I am initiating several new courses this year and now that I think of it, there is one that may be of interest to you: Creative Writing. You do indulge a little, don't you? I am afraid that the course may not attract many students so I should like to feel I can rely on the support of people like yourself, particularly in view of our conversation."

Whether this was a threat or a bargain, Mog could not decide, but she agreed to enroll. He smiled, satisfied, not knowing that his success was due to Mog's current preoccupation.

She might grow to like this place, Mog thought as she entered the library. It offered more latitude than school, by which she did not refer to the classes. These she could not assess, for so far little teaching had been attempted. Its attractions could not compete with the hypnotic powers of the register, which demanded meticulous entry of names, addresses, and enrollment numbers, an activity compared with which a public reading of the telephone directory would be a fun show. After such psychedelic entertainment there could only be a falling off and this was achieved by all the students describing their academic backgrounds. Mainly young men and women who after leaving school had decided to take A levels, and a sprinkling of apprehensive women, they looked very earnest and anxious to conform; but it was never too late for correction. Perhaps that was what Mr. Beadle meant by education's changing face.

Now that she had found an absorbing way to occupy her free time, the days were improving, Mog told herself as she took out her notebook. Retrospectively she would give last week a promising C plus (you had to keep up standards) whereas with the bonus of the nursery, today might merit a B. That depended on progress this afternoon. Unfortunately, since she had spent so much energy on Mr. Beadle, ideas might flag and to insure against such an unhappy predicament Mog dug into her haversack and extracted a Mars bar from her store.

If she went to this creative writing class she would have to take some actual writing; that seemed a fairly safe assumption. It was time she made a start on the book; a fortnight given to research was probably reasonable but not *productive*. To have something ready for the teacher provided a useful goal. Thinking further ahead, she decided to send the first three chapters to a publisher as soon as they were finished. That might lead to an advance on the rest. She was not sure whether to buy a typewriter first or the *Encyclopedia Britannica* for Ben.

She would do as Josephine suggested, find a basic model, some bread-and-butter fellow, and add the jam. Scribbling hurriedly, she began a synopsis: Marvin is a successful doctor. Obsessed with his work, he appears impervious to the charms of his colleague (or should she be his secretary? Josephine would do). He regards her with clinical detachment (especially when he is in his clinic. Ha!), and thinks of her not as a woman but as an arrangement of cells, organs, and all the rest of the apparatus that might one day require his professional touch. This is tested in chapter two when she falls and twists her leg (thigh? back? neck? shoulder? what else can you twist?). Is she right in sensing, as she lies in a semiswoon, that his professional mask has slipped for a second to reveal a strange, complex man who murmurs poetry as he massages the painful limb/organ, a man whose face, glimpsed through her misted contact lenses, betrays voluptuous thoughts?

"I don't like to make a criticism so early in the plot," a voice said, "but you will have to be more explicit about those voluptuous thoughts."

The young man with the variegated mane was at her shoulder. Mog closed the notebook. He sat down. Mog put the book in her haversack. He lifted the haversack, tested its weight, and replaced it on the table. Mog hung it from her shoulder.

"I suppose this is what is meant by a pregnant silence," he said. "You are dying to tell me that it is no business of mine to read what you are writing and I'm waiting to get in a word myself. You are right to say that it is no business of mine, but unhappily I have none of my own at the moment so I have to nick a bit of other people's. I didn't take much, only a glance."

He paused. Mog stared.

"I should not like you to think that a glance is all it deserves. I should be delighted to read more. In fact, a few stray words did catch my eye. Interesting, I thought, though not what I would have expected. What would you have expected? you ask. Now that is a difficult question. Delaying answer for a moment, I would just like to comment that I am taken aback by such diligent activity. Last time we met, you were attempting to read a book. Nothing wrong with that, you interrupt, and I agree, but on our second meeting you are scribbling away like words had gone out of fashion. Come to think of it, as far as your enunciation is concerned, they have."

Mog nodded, tired. It was amazing how he could go on. She discovered that she was picking at the cuticle of a nail, a habit she had noticed in Josephine. It must be catching.

"I know that you are anxious to hear my opinion on the frenetic way you apply yourself to tasks and, frankly, it is not wholly unreserved. I am impressed but regret that it leaves you so little time for conversation because I enjoyed the last one we had so much that I've spent days looking out for you, prepared to have another go. Thick of me, I suppose, but I'm like that."

"And you're learning to live with it," Mog said, getting up. He rose with her. "I was thinking of leaving myself."

Without speaking they walked together through the school and out of the main door. On the pavement the young man halted.

"I'll be seeing you around then," he said. "Take care." He crossed the street, turned, waved casually, strode to the corner, and disappeared.

Surprised, Mog walked after him. She had expected something different from that. In fact, before she had reached the main corridor, she had drafted it: HE: I'll see you home; SHE: No, thanks; HE: It's no trouble. I'm not pushed for time; SHE: In that case, you'll have to find some other way of occupying it.

However, that was too tame, so between the secretary's office and the pavement she had reworked it for inclusion in *An Anatomy of Passion,* chapter four.

. . . "It's time you and I had a talk, Josie," he said, his voice harsh with suppressed emotion. "There are things between us we have to get straight." She could feel her heart beating inside her backless evening gown which hugged her figure and fell in soft folds from her hips.

"Get into this car," he ordered; "I'm taking you home."

For a moment she struggled, then she was lifted, was carried toward the waiting pale blue Porsche, and almost fainting, she felt his body hard against hers, raw, masculine, and full of purpose. In the soft glow of the setting sun his finely chiselled profile was severe, uncompromising, and on the steering wheel his surgeon's hands were long-fingered, efficient, commanding. Josie's swiftly beating heart took another spin . . .

Rainbow Hair would be intrigued to read that paragraph, Mog thought, grinning. He would probably say that he would not have expected it while omitting to reveal what he would. But his parting was pretty sound. Also original. Keith would not have been capable of it; nor, for that matter, was he capable of loading her into his waiting Porsche. All he possessed was a go-cart, fallen into disuse. Seeing it once cased under polyethylene at the back of his father's garage, she had offered to buy it for Ben but he had declined on the grounds that it might come in useful for his son. He was seventeen at the time, an early age for entertaining hopes of paternity, especially in view of his slackness over the drill that precedes it. Comparing that with her improvised paragraph, Mog acknowledged how much fiction could improve on fact.

She had enjoyed composing that last bit; it almost made her appreciate Josephine's reaction to that other paragraph. As she walked over the derelict ground opposite the school, down numerous snickets and past the main shops, Mog reflected that writing your own stuff was more satisfactory than reading other people's; you could choose what went in. At risk of sounding immodest, she had to say that her writing might give as much pleasure to herself as it already had done to a wide, representative reading public: Josephine. Indeed, it had so much going for it that she might take it to excess. She was impatient to make a start. That evening.

Of course, trying to be objective, she could not guarantee how it would turn out; there had been the occasional venture that had been a fantabulous flop despite what she had put into it. Example, the forgettable Keith. But writing a book was different. You were in the driving seat and if a character was not coming up to scratch, you just rubbed him out.

One such character might well be her father, Mog said to herself as she entered the house. He was due to be zapped.

"He's wiring us up for a doorbell," her mother explained across the hole in the floor. "I've told him it's neither use nor ornament at the back and he'd be better out at the front, righting his chimes. People are always complaining they get 'Jingle Bells' when they've pressed for 'Silent Night.'"

"What can you expect from a second?" Cyril defended. "They should be grateful to have a choice."

Grace pulled the kitchen table to straddle the hole. "Tell him his tea's ready," she ordered.

"Tea's ready," Mog passed on from a distance of two feet.

Around the table the conversation lacked its usual vivacity; they were not brought up to date with Grace's jam making; there was no report on Cyril's new apprentice; and the condition of Great-aunt Edith's liver failed to get a mention. Being an opportunist, Ben took advantage of the silence to describe the goal he had scored that afternoon, demonstrating the deciding tackle with the help of Fred. After an unsolicited encore, he returned to his kipper unapplauded.

By a series of exaggerated hand and lip movements, Grace requested Ben to discover whether his father wanted a second cup of tea. Ben went through the same procedure, incorporating several grotesque additions. On the nod, Grace poured. Mog yawned. There were actual people dedicated to such farces for life! Such as mutes and mime artists and monks in a silent order. To prove that speech was still a viable alternative, she reported, "I'm going to join a Creative Writing class."

The announcement elicited no reaction, not even a digital spasm from Grace. Finally, after some painful contortions, Ben squeezed out a fart.

This was not good enough. Any minute rigor mortis would strike.

"The class is starting tomorrow evening. It should be useful, give me a few tips, since I'm going to write a book."

You would have thought that would raise a bit of interest. It is not every day that parents receive such news. Perhaps the response is usually indifference. In fact, all over the country at that very moment there could be people saying they were about to write a book and all the audience did was straighten the tea cosy (her mother), reach for another slice of bread (Ben), scratch their private parts (Fred), or gaze into the withered eye socket of a fish (her dad).

She would have to be more sensational.

"It will be a good chance to meet other people on the same jag, poets, television writers, people like that."

That worked. The company halted its activities but the habit of speech having lapsed, it was some time before anyone contrived to utter.

"I don't think I like that," Grace at last managed. "I mean, you don't know . . ."

"That's why I'm going, Mother."

Agitated, Grace scraped the fish bones on to the plate of bread. There followed indistinct, fractured sentences from which it was understood that poets and the rest were all mad, unwashed, drunken, and lawless and who, if television was anything to go by, went in for nothing but unbridled language and sex.

That seemed a good mix to Mog but this comment brought on further palpitations. Grace forecast that her peace of mind would be totally destroyed as she imagined what might happen to her daughter assailed by such temptations.

"You've a good line on depravity, Mother. I'll let you know how it matches up to the real thing."

Miserably, Grace appealed for support. "You just say to your father that I don't think you ought to go."

"I can't do that! My heart wouldn't be in the message, would it, Dad?"

Sliding back into the refuge of his hole, Mr. Dermot shook his head.

FOUR

It was a glutinous evening in late September and in that desolate hour between the last card punched in the factories and the first pint pulled in the bars, the town was still. Dusk was expected.

But in an unpretentious back street a beacon shone forth. Its light burnished the puddles in the unmetalled car park; its beams sought out JANICE LOVES TONY inside the bus shelter; its radiance made a fairyland of the corporation tip; its iridescence softened the contours of warehouses, made sculptures of scaffolding, created collages of litter, and discovered poetry in the damp patches beside the urinal. All over Nathaniel Chubb the lamps had been switched on.

And at their signal the town stirred. Memories were revived of spare parts at a premium in Car Maintenance classes and men rushed on to the streets, added bolts to bumpers, stuck down windshield wipers, and locked up spare tires; remembering the popularity of Economical Cookery, managers raced back to their shops and began stripping their shelves; and anticipating the unleashed enthusiasm of flower arrangers, the park attendant collected up chicken wire behind which to corral his blooms. Mr. Beadle's vision of a community college that entered the lives of every member of its catchment had come to pass.

Except that there were parts of it that remained ignored. Elbowing past lines of people enrolling for House Plantology, Zip Insertion Techniques, Christmas Tree Decorating, Inexpensive Party Menus (designed for the unemployed), and all the unimaginable activities that demonstrated the Principal's notion of recreation, Mog searched for the other half of his vision: learning in the true sense of the word.

There were not many takers for it that evening and those engaged to conduct it sat dismally underneath the paper banners that advertised their wares. Though some attempted badinage with a neighbor, most of them were hunched over their tables, doodling across the empty columns of their registers or gazing forlornly toward the other end of the hall and its teeming mob. Mog thought this a mistake. You did not get anywhere if you sat around waiting for something to happen; you had to get off your bum and on to the street. Move in where the action was and start rustling yourself.

She put this to Elizabethan Drama. "In the first place, you'll never pull in the crowds with a title like that. It needs to hit them where they live. I mean, Elizabethan Drama has got everything. You ought to call it 'Murder, Fornication, and Incest, Elizabethan Style.' I bet if you went along those lines up there and told them it was all a matter of 'rank sweat in a hot semen bed,' you'd get a full house."

"According to *Hamlet* it is 'rank sweat of an enseamed bed,' " the other corrected.

At which, Mog gave him up. Anyone so pedantic deserved an empty register.

Two tables further on, the sign CREATIVE WRITING wagged in the draft. Clipped to it was a note from Myrtle: "Tutor, Nan Glen, author," with the helpful gloss "of books." Mog homed in.

The author who wrote books was, however, otherwise employed fitting in a brief nap. This gave Mog the opportunity for thorough appraisal. She had never met an author before. The nearest she had come to one was in the office of the town's weekly free paper whose clerk, between taking in advertisements, spent his time plagiarizing the local radio for dog ends of news. As a guide to the temperament, life-style, etc. of a writer, he was unreliable. Nor did the specimen in front of her offer many clues. Though she slept with her mouth open there were no fumes of whiskey; more garlic, Mog thought, taking a discreet sniff. Nothing in her face suggested debauchery, though perhaps that would be noticeable only when pursued to excess. No volume or much-worked typescript bulged from her clothing, which itself was unremarkable except for the hi-tech boots. All this was disappointing. But what Mog knew she could depend on was an immaculate syntax, an elegant style, and a breathtaking luminosity of expression.

"I'm buggered," the woman said, opening an eye.

Occasionally, in the interest of clarity, something has to go.

"Any particular reason?" Mog asked.

"Yes, the car conked out and I had to take to the hoof."

Mog smiled bravely.

"I've got a pencil," she said as the woman began to stir up the entrails of a carrier bag.

The other accepted this gratefully, remarking that she could never find anything to write with and, opening the register, asked for Mog's name. She had several shots at it, displaying an ingenuity that was astonishing. When they had reached an agreement on the surname, Mog informed her there were two *a*'s in Margaret, but if she preferred she could just put down Mog.

Nan Glen scratched that in with relief. "I'm a rotten speller," she said with the air of one making an incredible confession. "It's a good thing I'm not in charge of O level

Language. Mind you, I shan't be taking this course if no more enroll. You're number five and we need ten for a . . . what's it?"

"Quorum," Mog supplied.

"That's right. All the same, I am opening the class in room seventeen at half past eight. See what you are all interested in. No reason to tackle it at half cock, even if the class may fold in a couple of weeks."

Mog smiled, approving.

"Not that I'm all that bothered, but I need the bread, such as it is. I write novels," Nan Glen confided as if that explained all.

Mog found that surprising. Perhaps if you went into writing novels full time there were a lot of hidden expenses that soaked up the cash. She would have to inquire about that. However, the chance would not occur if the class were withdrawn.

"I'll see if I can persuade a few others to join," she said.

"I don't altogether like the idea of your pimping for me. It is not an easy job proselytizing artistic endeavor and apart from the effort required, people have an understandable reticence about exposing their feelings on paper."

Though the expression had improved, Mog could not agree with the opinion. There must be scores of people dying to see their names in print.

Three men waiting to register for body-building loudly denied this. In fact, they assured her that half the town would pay any money to keep their names out of it. It caused a lot of unnecessary complications with the wife or the boss. Description became animated, but when Mog had corrected the misunderstanding and told them they had marvelous copy for the class, they immediately experienced the writer's nightmare and dried up.

Saying that she would bear them in mind, a promise that brought the weediest guy out in a sweat, Mog passed on.

She had fifteen minutes before the class began, during which she could keep an eye open for potential customers for Nan Glen while drafting the next paragraph of the novel. In the last twenty-four hours ideas had come in so fast that she had had trouble getting them down. A student had been cajoled to hand over his notes from the day's classes, in return for the service in the future, so she had written all day, had done the second chapter and was well into the third. Since the first had been dashed off before going to bed the previous evening, Mog calculated that she could have chapters one, two, and three finished, copied, and in the post by the next afternoon.

. . . Automatically she typed on,

Mog continued chapter three as she strode down the corridor,

> . . . trying to concentrate upon the letters as they advanced across the handmade paper with his beautiful monogram and stylishly printed address, but they were a blur. On the other side of the door which separated her office from the consulting room she could hear his voice speaking in low, intimate tones. "Make sure that you send Miss Juliet Bellisimo into me immediately," he had said in a way that told her the famous model was more than a patient. He had seemed not to notice Josie as he spoke, whereas yesterday he had complimented her on her new cardigan, pretty, he had said, and matching her eyes. She had risen early this morning and blow-waved her hair . . .

"I hesitate to distract an author in the throes of composition," a voice interrupted, "but I was wondering if I might solicit a word. No, I suppose not. You are not to be tempted into idle prattle; I deduce that from your glare.

"How did I know you were engaged in a literary workout? you ask me," Rainbow Hair continued. "I'll tell you: by the intense expression and the frantic movement of the lips. Is the young woman drunk, stoned, or round the twist? I questioned myself. Then suddenly revelation came in what you would describe as a blinding flash. I am left not quite speechless, as you may have noticed, but still breathless. With admiration. Or could it be the sprint necessary to catch you up?"

He paused. "Okay, don't bother to comment. It must be hard, descending to the level of the masses. On the other hand, if you did feel inclined to give inspiration a rest, you might like to join me in a dose of Noreen's tea."

"No, thanks."

"A word, at last! Nay, two! Watch it, my girl; you might get hooked. Why, no? You would be absolutely safe. I am free from the more common germs: Asian flu, foot-and-mouth disease, cowpox, bubonic plague. Nor should I pass on my secret ailments: housemaid's knee, tennis elbow, ballerina's toe, huntsman's crotch . . ."

"Or disc jockey jaw?"

"Nice; and you've doubled your word score. Sorry about the rhyme; it must be the company I'm trying to keep."

"Look, do you *mind?* I've just enrolled for the Creative Writing class . . ."

"So Denis tells me. He's the guy standing over there, the one dredging his nose. A sort of peripatetic mate of mine, despite the odd unsavory habit."

". . . and the course tutor wants us back," checking her watch, "in less than ten minutes. But we haven't a quorum yet. I was on my way to the cafeteria to see if I could drum up any interest."

"A very worthy reason for declining the school brew. And I do not think you need be anxious about the quorum. Previously I would have held out no hope but you've managed to persuade the Beadle to start a day nursery, haven't you? Mega amazing. With your track record, eight minutes gives you a fair chance to haul a few bodies into a class."

"But I'm passing up the chance to quip briskly, 'And I suppose you think you can supply one,' " she quoted him.

He laughed. " ' "You anticipate," he answered suavely.' Christ! This is beginning to sound like conversations in those damned books you read! I'm off. Have fun!"

She wondered how he knew about the nursery and how he was able to imitate the style of books he had claimed were not to his taste, but anyone who could combine that design of hair with his kind of speech was unpredictable. She might have found him interesting if she had not given up men. Reflecting on this, Mog walked into the cafeteria.

As Mr. Beadle explained in the school prospectus, this was the social center until the common room was built, part of the school extension that remained but a dream on the drawing board mainly because its realization meant digging up two streets. Addressing himself to adult evening students, he apologized for the cafeteria's shortcomings but was confident that they would find it the place to which they naturally gravitated, seeking the stimulus of informal discussion, the intangible benefits of reciprocal experience, and the opportunity to pool their maturity of understanding and knowledge without stint. As yet, however, the cafeteria's shortcomings outweighed its intangible benefits and there was only one occupant who had naturally gravitated to the place.

He was bent over the table and appeared to be writing, an encouraging sign that he might be interested in the class, and he was so engrossed in his art that he did not look up when Mog approached.

The art the man was engaged in at that moment was original but in a sense parasitic. He had a newspaper and with an assortment of felt-tipped pens was applying clothes to a buxom woman who, in spite of being issued with a bikini nicked from a dwarf, was taking the inconvenience in good part.

"It shouldn't be allowed," he stated, looking up.

Mog agreed. Pleased to have found a man committed to reforming a basic view of her sex, she discussed the implications of the photograph, its effects upon women in general and upon the model herself, its central position in the sexist philosophy, and less important but still worth mentioning, its anatomical inaccuracy for few women possess such a distorted shape.

"That's right," the man agreed, hanging a shopping basket in the model's hand. "All trollops. It's disgusting."

This answer suggested that he had not quite followed her argument but clarification could wait. "Would you be interested in joining a class?" she asked.

The man filled the shopping basket with packets of detergent before replying. "I might," he said at last. "All depends."

"You wouldn't have to pay," she told him quickly. "It says old-age pensioners can join for free."

"I know that, young woman," he snapped. "Been to night school more often than you've had hot dinners. Comes in handy in the winter months."

A purist would have winced at this reason for education, but Mog's sensibilities were more robust. "Fine. It's a course on creative writing. Starts tonight. Okay?"

"I'm not fussy, since it's coming on to rain. I don't mind looking in."

"I'll give you a hand with your luggage," and carrying three of his six plastic bags, Mog led him to the class. Another name for the register was a good haul in under eight minutes and she hoped Nan Glen would appreciate it. She would probably not notice the voluminous overcoat, string belt, and rubber boots; and if people complained of asphyxiation, they could open a window to get rid of the pong.

Mr. Beadle's fertility when providing evening courses was not inhibited by petty deficiencies of accommodation. Room seventeen was a graveyard for furniture and the repository for cleaners' mops. However, it was not the environment that mattered, Mog reminded herself; it was the people. But they looked a boring lot. There were no bare feet or velvet suits and the one in leathers was nothing new. Mog comforted herself that their appearance was irrelevant; the important thing was what they produced.

It appeared that Nan Glen was equally indulgent. She did not flinch as she wrote Albert's name in the register—perhaps her olfactory organs were faulty—but Mog noted that she had trouble on sighting a woman's tulle hat. This was momentary; she refocused into the far distance, quickly enumerated her credentials for such employment, waved a number of books, and, articulation refreshed by her nap, defined policy: she did not regard herself as teacher but supervisor; this was a support group not a class and would be shaped by their needs and problems. Meanwhile she would like to hear about the writing each one of them did.

This invitation was not accepted with enthusiasm. Albert set about another photograph with his felt tips; the young man in leathers took out his receipt of enrollment and began a feverish search for inspiration; the rest looked shifty. This was puzzling. Mog filled her lungs.

"What about you, Mrs. Lewis?" Nan Glen asked a woman in the front row.

Nervously picking at the cuff of her hand-knitted cardigan, Mrs. Lewis confessed that she had produced nothing to date, but her sister wrote stories.

"Why didn't you bring her along?" Mog asked.

"She's looking after the children."

Wherever you turn there are women looking after one another's children, Mog thought to herself; but before she could inquire how Mr. Lewis was occupied, Nan Glen had pointed to Denis, Rainbow Hair's peripatetic mate, who was spread out at the back.

To ensure a satisfactory standard of voice production, Denis checked on a nostril then said that he thought he would write for TV. "I'm very visual," he explained, unlatching another button of his shirt. "And I've got the ideas, the plots, like. Only it's the padding that gets me. So I reckoned if I sketched them in and somebody wouldn't mind filling them out? I wouldn't object to sharing the credit."

"Now isn't that a good idea?" the woman in the tulle and petal cloche enthused, omitting to offer her services. "I like a good serial on the TV myself, but generally it's Mr. Kitson who keeps it on, he says for the company. I'm otherwise occupied." She smiled; the hat tilted coyly. "You see, I have a different lover every night."

There was no rush to congratulate. Glances were exchanged. Mog wondered whether a few questions on method of recruitment and logistics of organization would be misunderstood.

"Trollop," Albert gave his verdict, and began to sheet up another model.

"Did he write love stories? I thought his books are all about clergymen. It's Romances I'm interested in, Mrs. Glen."

"Miss."

"Oh, sorry. And sometimes I've thought, why not do one myself? That is when the library is running out."

Disappointed, the class sighed. Nan Glen yanked off her boots. Albert selected another felt tip. The young man in leathers scrutinized his enrollment slip. Less aggressively decked out in a gray suit and white shirt, the last man in the class frowned at his notebook.

"Which reminds me," Nan Glen said. "I should like you all to have something to read to us next week. Select any form you prefer, but I suggest a piece of dialogue from you, Denis. And if you can't think of anything," she soothed Mrs. Lewis's alarm, "write about an incident you have experienced with your children."

"I'd do a Romance," Mrs. Kitson reminded them, "if I had a plot."

It was time, Mog decided, to get in where the action was. "Do you mean one like *Body Heat* or *Torrid Love?*"

"Oh, I haven't read those, but you soon forget the title, don't you? That doesn't matter, does it? I mean, you know what you're going to get. That's one of the lovely things about them." The hat flapped, signaling welcome. Mrs. Kitson had found a friend.

"I can give you a plot." The woman needed help. For someone who had promised to shape the course to their needs, Nan Glen was a bit slow. "What about a secretary, call her something like Crystal, who works in a travel agency and her boss, the owner of a big chain including an airline, takes her with him on a business trip to open a new office, somewhere like Morocco, and leaves her alone one afternoon when she is caught up in the white slave traffic."

"What an imagination! Do you mind if I take that down? You don't meet an idea like that every day, do you?" Mrs. Kitson beamed, addressing the rest.

They seemed inclined to agree with her. In fact, their expressions conveyed that the infrequency of the meeting occasioned relief. But once was enough for one of them. He was the young man in leathers. As Mrs. Kitson reached for her notebook and Nan Glen for tobacco, he rose, stumbled to the front, and, holding his enrollment receipt like an exorcizing crucifix, explained that he thought he must be in the wrong class. "I'd hoped for the new Maths."

"What's wrong with here?" Albert demanded. "It don't let in wet."

"It's the Maths I signed for," the other wailed. "Look, that's what it says," prodding the slip.

This diversion afforded Denis the opportunity to move to the desk next to Mog. "I like that white-slave trader bit," he told her and, cackling, added a nudge and a wink.

"But I haven't been to Morocco," Mrs. Kitson worried, foreseeing a snag.

Mog advised her to study the travel brochures.

Again, Mrs. Kitson was impressed. "That's the lovely thing about love stories, isn't it? They take you to such exciting places."

Mrs. Lewis complained that her family could only afford to visit her parents in Sutton-on-Sea.

"That's right!" Mrs. Kitson agreed. "When you're stuck at home, it's one way of traveling. But that is nothing compared to the story. In the end, no matter what happens, they come together. True love. That's nice."

There was a pause. The woman's fervor was daunting. The man in the suit glanced toward the top desk as if hoping to encourage Nan Glen's slight grasp of her supervisory function, but she was supporting Leathers to the door. Temporarily assuming her role, he asked if Mrs. Kitson was a sales representative.

"Whatever gave you that idea? I'm just a plain housewife. I've never gone out to work. I believe it is my job to see the home is comfy and meals on the table for Mr. Kitson."

"Quite right, too," Albert said.

"I've got it down as far as Morocco." She turned to Mog, pen at the ready. "But there has to be a twist. We can't have him rescuing her from the Arab without some complications."

The woman's analysis of her reading matter deserved at least a B, Mog decided, noting that Nan Glen had muzzled her face in her bag. Either it was time for her oats or the class had sent her autistic.

"What do you suggest?" Mrs. Kitson prompted.

Mog regretted her generous assistance. One day, sorting out people would get her into trouble. "He could have a wife already," she suggested wildly. "Like one in a psychiatric ward or something."

Mrs. Kitson was delighted but was not sure whether that was grounds for divorce.

At last emerging from her bag with a tin of tobacco and papers, Nan Glen made a contribution. "Is your echo of *Jane Eyre* deliberate?" she asked Mog. "You remember Mr. Rochester's mad wife?"

Mog's answer was prevented by sighs from the other women and their chorus expressing lifelong attachment to the said book.

Albert, however, had reservations. Having watched it on television, he judged there were bad mistakes. That Mr. Rochester should never have tried to rescue that batty wife of his but let her frizzle straight off, nor should he have got mixed up with that Jane. She was a proper little upstart. He would have been well advised to lock her up in the attic as well.

Mrs. Kitson paled. "But Mr. Rochester could never do anything like that! He loved her!"

"He ought to have known better," the other answered, scathing. "A grown man like him!"

For someone who was just looking in, Albert was participating to excess. He was also an argument for improved ventilation. Anxious to convey these points, Mog tried to gain Nan Glen's attention, but Mrs. Kitson had moved in to attack.

"It's because he was a grown man that he knew what was good for him," she pronounced vigorously. "She was only a frail little thing but she loved him with the strength of steel and no man can do better than that."

"What evidence have you for that statement?" the suited man asked.

Mrs. Kitson ignored him. "When she heard his voice calling in the night, she knew he needed her and without a moment's hesitation she went to him. And what did she find?" She drew out a handkerchief. "She found a man, blind and maimed; but that only made her love him more, so she nursed him like a mother. Because he had *suffered,* and he loved Jane with every fiber of his being."

"Can that include deception?" Nan Glen mused. "I refer to his attempt at bigamous marriage with her."

Taken off guard, Mrs. Kitson swallowed, then adopted a conciliatory tone in deference to the other's position. "Well, it wasn't really the right thing to do since bigamy is illegal."

"It was not the illegality I was thinking of."

"He only tried it on because he loved her," Mrs. Kitson defended. "It's proof how much he did. He had to have her, whether it was right or wrong. There aren't many men who would do that."

"You'd be surprised," Denis tittered.

"Can you quote the figures?" the gray suit asked.

Mrs. Kitson raised a hand as if appealing against a foul. As an exponent of the best-loved Romance in the canon, she was not doing too well. Then she recovered. "Figures! Statistics! That's all some men can think about. But there are others interested in more than that. Real men. We women can recognize one when we see him. And so could Jane."

"Me Tarzan; you Jane," Denis interpolated.

Mrs. Kitson froze him. "And in the end, she gets her reward!" She rested, triumphant.

"Harlot!" Albert declared loudly, waving a plastic bag.

For a second his target remained ambiguous. Mrs. Kitson's nostrils pinched. Then, pushing back her chair, she hissed above him, "You don't know what I'm talking about. I'm talking about LOVE."

Undismayed, he sucked in his cheeks, slapped his tongue over his lips, and set up a thin treble:

> *"In the twilight you talk about love,*
> *And weep at its pain."*

"We know what that is, if you don't." Mrs. Kitson's voice struck above him while she gestured toward Mog, Mrs. Lewis, and Nan Glen. "It's going through hell and high water if necessary, and Jane knew that. She was only an inexperienced slip of a girl, but she knew."

"While you beg me to light up the stars," Albert continued, getting into the swing of it, volume increasing. *"And hold back the rain."*

"Because of what he did, she wandered over the countryside like a pauper. . . ."

"But I tell you my lips cannot move." Amplifier going full blast.

". . . All the same, she could forgive." Shrieking counterpoint.

"To love's soft refrain."

". . . So in the end she has a husband, a home, and a child, what every woman wants." Brandishing her handbag.

"Yet the tears I will wipe from your cheeks,

"Then—" Dramatic pause.

"And let me remind you." Mrs. Kitson's voice was magnified another twenty decibels; the handbag punched the air. "However hard she is pressed, she'll not have any of it till he's free to marry her and she's sure of her man."

"Then you'll love me again."

Albert's last line, delivered in a choking whisper, deprived Mrs. Kitson's conclusion of the expected musical backing. Hence it rang above the noise of people walking down the corridor and was clearly heard by those already clustered

around the door. The group became aware of faces squashed
against the glass. There was an uncomfortable silence.

"Well, that seems a good moment to finish," Nan Glen said,
groping for her boots. "I am pleased we were able to fit in a
meeting after enrollment. It has been a useful half hour. Thank
you all for making such lively contributions." Stowing cigarette butts in a pocket, she added bravely, "I look forward to
seeing you again next week."

Mog walked through the school. The last students to enroll
were with Myrtle, who was hurrying to relieve them of their
money before they could change their minds; a few others
were hanging about the main hall trying to gain the attention
of members of staff who, pretending blindness, were edging
away. Among them, the caretaker, bemused by an evening's
resort to hip flask, was puzzling out the trick of folding up
tables while keeping an eye on an Alsatian brought along as an
exhibit by an aspiring dog handler.

Outside, the glow from Nathaniel Chubb was dimmed, but
across the patch of waste ground opposite, the Drayman's
Arms was providing a satisfactory alternative. On the path
that linked the two institutions Nan Glen could be observed
scurrying as if making for base.

"She looked like she needed one," Denis commented, joining Mog on the pavement. "After that hag in the hat. Got
possibilities, hasn't she? Be fanciable if she weren't getting on."

"You mean Mrs. Kitson?"

"Lay off! Nan Glen. Mid-thirties, I'd say. Mind you, there
are still some that can push the pace even at that age, not that
I've been there," adding quickly to forestall accusations of neglect, "so far."

"Where're you going, then?" he asked, accompanying her
down the street.

"Home."

When he had offered to take her, she would recite the appropriate dialogue ending, "In that case, you'll have to find some other way of occupying your time."

"Going to dash off a story like you gave that woman? I wouldn't have wasted it on her. The way she went on! Creepy. Real men! She wouldn't recognize one if she saw him," Denis sneered, indignant.

Mog laughed. "Perhaps she was confused by your neck chain."

"Do you mind? All she's happy with is somebody too beaten up to offer resistance. Nursing him like a mother! It's humiliating. Makes you feel for that bloke Rochester, it does."

Mog was intrigued. In her sophomore year, reading the book had occasioned tears, Josephine's exceptionally copious. "I never thought of it like that."

"Well, you wouldn't, but I'm seeing it from the man's point of view and it's not right. I mean, if it's a hospital job you can't expect anything else, but on a regular basis it's insulting. What man wants to be babied? That's not what he's there for, is it?"

It was a question that, generally applied, Mog found difficult to answer; but what Denis was there for at that moment was less obscure. Throughout his last paragraph, as if to give emphasis to his argument, he had kept up a good deal of thigh, hip, and arm contact, a remarkable feat to combine with walking, and it reached gold medal standards when, in an attempt to elude him, Mog adopted a zigzagging course.

"Mind you," Denis added, gliding into step as she took a bend, "I wouldn't say no if it was you seeing to me."

"Sorry; that's not my style." When they reached the next corner she would see him off.

"I didn't think it was. You want a bit more action."

To demonstrate his willingness to provide this, Denis flung out an arm like a grappling iron and secured her to him. This arrangement fixed their tacking progress to an ungainly plod but it was not altogether uncomfortable. Mog decided that being tethered to Denis was not an issue she wished to raise. She was tired: it had been a busy day.

"So what're you waiting for?" he demanded, close to her ear.

"Action man?" she hazarded. Denis chuckled.

Mog noticed they had passed the corner. As soon as the right moment came, she would wriggle free.

"No hassle," he assured her, increasing his grip.

Men like him have an incredible swagger, Mog concluded from the evidence of one sample. All he thinks he has to do is put an arm around her waist! Keith did not think that. In fact, he never put an arm anywhere except in his own coat sleeve, then left the hand dangling or plugged into a pocket out of harm's way.

While he had thoughts. Voluptuous thoughts. Eternally in my—

Something of that kind seemed to be affecting Denis, for his hand, having burrowed as far as her sweatshirt, was now blundering around searching for the welt. Mog shivered.

"You're cold. Want to swap? This jacket is thicker than your anorak."

Though a rather conventional opening for a strip, it was redeemed by originality in choice of place—alongside the petrol pumps in the middle of town. Under the lamps in the garage forecourt his complexion was sallow; she had not noticed what shade of olive or bronze it had assumed under the school lights.

He was unbuttoning his jacket with his free hand.

"Don't worry. I'm all right."

It was time for her to go. Examining the models in the showroom, he had slowed their pace but his arm was still a restraint.

"I could do with a car. It has its uses." He sniggered. "Or a small van."

Both were an improvement on a go-cart, especially when troubled by voluptuous thoughts. Again Mog shivered.

"Christ! You must be catching cold, woman." He stopped, his attention wholly on her. "You ought to wear more," he reproved, solicitous.

> . . . They were standing in shadow so the full depth of his gaze was concealed by the strong jutting brow, but the low crepuscular beams of the evening sun revealed cheeks and mouth agitated with an emotion whose agony wrenched at her heart. Then murmurs escaped him and above the rising wind which twitched the leaves of the laurels she heard him say, "I will cherish her. I will guard. No evil will touch her, for is she not as my own flesh?" The words were spoken with the passion and solemnity of an oath pronounced before his Maker, then as the first livid lights cracked in the sky Mr. Rochester shuddered, looked down at the slight form he held in his arms and said, "The weather changes, Jane, my darling. Come, we must retire indoors" . . .

Opening his jacket, he held it around her and, pulled close, she was guided along the path. "Come on, let's take a turn in the old park," Denis said to her, "and find some warm."

Mog stopped. The park he referred to was disused, sliced by a motorway; the warmth, a derelict bandstand, and a few mangy shrubs. She slid from his arm.

"I'm sorry, but I've a lot of work to do before tomorrow."

Then she turned and strode away.

Because he had misinterpreted her shivers, which had nothing to do with catching cold. Because the park was smelly. Because she had decided against men. Because Keith had never made that kind of proposal.

No wonder she felt rotten. What she was suffering from was misery, third degree. The evening had started well enough,

Mog reminded herself as she entered her street, then it had gradually degenerated until it was a total mess. Somewhere along the line she suspected it was that Mrs. Kitson's fault. She would sort that out later.

So, distracted, she had the key in the lock before she remembered. Her mother would be in the living room in front of the television; she would have the sound turned down, listening for the worst. It would not do to disappoint her. Mog sighed. She felt exhausted and eight feet of path, one doormat, and one step did not offer much scope. But there were three empty milk bottles.

One important principle, Mog told herself as she knocked these over, is that however bushed you are (giggling loudly, stumbling over the mat, and lunging into the door), you have to keep a grip on essentials (running down the path and banging the gate). Then she tiptoed back and let herself into the house.

Having thus satisfied her mother's expectations, Mog felt better. Also, you should always keep your options open. He was, as he said, very visual.

FIVE

"You've got a letter," Ben told her, his mouth full of toast. "It's from a magazine; that's printed on the flap. And it was posted in London."

"What does it say inside?"

"It's addressed to you! I don't go reading other people's letters. I mean, it's not a card, is it? It's stuck down." A boy with principles.

These became strained when Mog opened the envelope and drew out a check.

"I wish I could write letters that were published. I could do with some cash," he mourned.

"What for?"

Starting modestly with roller skates, Ben moved on to an air gun, wondered whether the money would run to a music center, and, to demonstrate that his thoughts were not entirely selfish, considered a new collar for Fred.

"It's only three pounds."

"That would be a start."

There are many kinds of romance, Mog reflected. "You can have it," she said.

Ben's thanks took the form of hollering praise to the Spurs and the emission of wind.

"Well, isn't that nice?" Grace said, referring to the gift. "Now you just give our Maggie a kiss."

"I'll pass that up," Mog granted, seeing his horror.

"It was conscience money," she explained to Josephine later. "The idea in the letter was okay but the correspondent turned out a twit. I felt I'd let women down because I'd made her sound so stupid."

"Why not, if she was?"

"Jo, I invented her. The girl doesn't exist."

"In that case, what's your problem?"

Sometimes Mog had the impression that she failed to communicate, but she was willing to have another go. Sensing this, Josephine asked, "How's the book?"

Mog brought her up-to-date: first three chapters posted to publisher and awaiting response; next chapters on the drawing board but production slowed down in the last three weeks owing to a number of difficulties not yet resolved.

Knowing that these were about to be visited upon her, Josephine glanced around the cafeteria in the hope of spotting a distraction. None presented itself.

"You see, Jo, one thing is I've reached the point where the heroine should be considering the fella's potential."

"You mean you've got to a dirty bit?" the other asked, perking up.

"Can't you think of anything else?"

"It's you writing the book," Josephine defended.

"I'm talking about what he's got going for him and how she is feeling, attracted to him in a way and yet holding off. It's got to be subtle."

"Well, yuss," she agreed, taking out a bottle of nail polish and unscrewing the cap.

"Especially since, so far, he's a pain."

"In that case, she'd be better off without," Josephine advised, pumping the brush.

Mog sighed. Conversation with Josephine could be exasperating on occasions. "You may be right, but according to the plot she has to hang on because really she thinks he's ace."

"Takes all sorts," depositing a blob of pearlized lacquer on a thumbnail.

You can go so wrong expecting help from a friend, Mog reminded herself, grinding her teeth. What with Mrs. Kitson and Denis, that first writing class had thrown up a number of issues she would have liked to discuss but there had been no opportunity at subsequent meetings, devoted mainly to the serious man's poetry and the implausible autobiography of the timid Mrs. Lewis. In any case, for the most intimate questions, they were an unsuitable audience. As, it seemed, was this. However, Mog persevered.

"Jo, have you ever thought out this love bit?"

The response to that was more satisfactory. Josephine paused in midstroke. "What love bit? At the moment there's nothing to think out. Haven't you noticed?" She gestured around them, spraying the table with Wanton Flame. "They aren't exactly lining up."

Mog had to agree but wished that, when discussing principles, Josephine would keep to the general rather than the particular.

"It's the particular I'm interested in."

"Right," Mog conceded. You had to make an effort with Jo when she was in an uncooperative mood. "Suppose some guy turned up and you went for him, would you nurse him like a mother if necessary, or go through hell and high water for him, or forgive him if he attempted bigamy with you, or go back to him after he had caused you to wander round the countryside like a pauper?"

"Is that what she does in your book? I like it! Quite honestly, Mog, I never imagined you could think up anything like that!"

"That's *Jane Eyre,*" Mog snapped. Any minute now and she would give up. "Don't you remember?"

"I remember Mr. Rochester." She gazed into the middle distance, lips parted; then added, nostalgic, "He was a man and a half."

And better left out of the conversation, Mog groaned to herself. A pity she had ignored Josephine's previous form. If she were not careful, soon the table would be awash. Further talk on this line was pointless; she could predict exactly how it would go: MOG: So would you? JO: (still vacant) What? MOG: Do all that for a man? JO: Well, she did, didn't she? MOG: But, Jo, that's no argument. Jane Eyre didn't *exist.*

"But Mr. Rochester didn't exist," Josephine observed sadly, coming up for air. "He is in a *book.*" Recovery was faster than it had been in her sophomore year. It must be her age, Mog decided, or the discouraging environment. "All the same, if anyone like him showed up, I don't reckon I should have any trouble with the love bit. And you needn't start objecting to that, because it's different for you; you've given up men." The reminder was irritating. "All you have to worry about is whether your heroine can fall in love with a jerk, whereas I'm worried because at the moment I just might."

Mog giggled.

"I'm serious. There's no telling what might happen when you've been hanging about. Look at our Glenda. After three months' knitting in front of the TV she ends up with a creep with false teeth selling insurance. I mean, why did it have to be insurance? And it's years since I finished with Robin."

"Months," Mog corrected in the hope of combating pessimism. It might be infectious.

"Could be, but I'm saying how it *feels.* I don't like to admit this, Mog, particularly after what I said about Robin, but I do miss having him about."

Mog thought that was not surprising since his bulk was his most memorable feature.

Josephine was not disposed to laugh. "But why should I, when it was me lost interest? Though I was gone on him at first, I really was. But it isn't only him; it's anybody. What gets me down is being without. As far as I'm concerned, life without a bloke is like a cafeteria dinner without the chips."

After that, talk lapsed.

Which was not much of a loss, Mog told herself. The conversation had been no use. She might have guessed that Josephine would be infatuated with a Mr. Rochester; during a male recession you would expect her discrimination to be up the creek. It was a waste of time to hope for anything else. In any case, though opinion polls gave you the key to other people's behavior, they offered no guidance for your own.

She would have to attempt a systematic breakdown of the problem. It was curious that up to now she had avoided that, letting her thoughts revolve unchecked until she was suffering from vertigo. The result was mental staleness, energy used up but nothing produced. This was bound to make you miserable. Perhaps if she could pull the mess into shape, issues would be clearer and the next chapters would take off.

Spreading her belongings over three chairs and a table in the library, its emptiness suggesting that the Beadle gospel of learning in the true sense of the word had not yet caught on, Mog found a clean page in her notebook, headed it: LOVE, SOME THOUGHTS AND QUERIES, and began.

1. Can't forget Mrs. Kitson's description of Jane Eyre. *Doesn't it apply to most heroines in our Glenda's library books?*

2. Mrs. Kitson does not seem bothered by the fact that Jane puts up with Mr. Rochester when he is cruel to her (lets her think he is getting married to someone else). Also, she doesn't like flashy gear but she lets Mr. R. buy new dresses for her.

She even continues to like Mr. R. after he has tried bigamy with her. (Nan Glen disapproved because it was deceit.) And the way J.E. calls him Master all the time makes you sick. I expect Mrs. Kitson laps that up! I think he's a selfish prat. *Is it necessary for a woman to behave like that?*

3. Mrs. Kitson says that everything J.E. does proves that she loves him. Suppose a woman can't compete with Jane Eyre as above, *does that mean she will never fall in love?*

4. *Does an author of a Romance have to be in love herself to write it?*

5. *What are the criteria for nipping into the park?* Stupid question. Answer: the right vibes. What are they? Anyway, they are not necessarily the same as love.

6. *Why did I start this book?* I've given up men! Because it was a way of filling in spare time resulting from that decision. Also, I need some capital. I can enjoy the luxury of not being mercenary when I have collected a few essentials: Raster Blaster, fashion boots, dictaphone, sag bag.

7. *What the hell IS love?*

"Good question," Rainbow Hair said, pulling up a chair opposite her. "Sorry. Just picked up the odd word."

"One of these days you'll pick up something and be really sorry." She was annoyed by the insipid answer.

"I'm willing to take the risk. But being an optimist I don't expect to regret what I might pick up."

Mog decided this was the moment to stare him out.

She saw that the spikes round his head had been brushed flat. He was no longer sporting plumage, but petals; not hair, but a close-fitting cap. Home grown. With many more like him about, Mrs. Kitson's milliner would be out of business.

"Lost in thought?" he demanded. "Like some food for it? Shall we postpone the metaphorical and start with the literal?

i.e., a Mars bar? Haven't I observed that you have a certain fondness? Want half?"

It seemed childish to decline. Mog added a comment on the new abbreviated and interrogatory style.

"Why stick to the previous one when it was ineffective? And aren't questions the in thing this lunch hour?" He nodded towards her notes, then with a flamboyant gesture placed a Mars bar on the table, went through his pockets, discovered a nail file and polished it on a sleeve. "Mind if I carve? This is a damned lively little weapon, ma'am," trying the edge on his thumb, "and I'll not answer for the consequences in another's hand."

It was hard to suppress a laugh but she had already over-done the encouragement in accepting the chocolate.

"Am I right in deducing that you have problems with the book? When you write something like that don't you simply go along with the requirements and no questions asked?"

"I've got seven."

"So I see. No, if you were thinking of handing them over for me to read, don't trouble. During interviews, in order to cor-rect misjudgments that have been furtively scribbled about me, I have perfected the skill of reading upside down."

Mog wished that the Mars bar had been slapstick custard pie, guaranteed adhesive on impact. There was no point now in closing the notebook.

"Would you like to test SOME THOUGHTS AND QUERIES on me? Right. I'd agree that most heroines in your library books have similarities with Jane Eyre. The original model, no doubt. Yes, I've been catching up with your reading matter. Let's see. Question two gets an emphatic no; behaving like Jane Eyre if a woman fancies a man is not only unnecessary but, in my view, distinctly no go. Other descriptions spring to mind but I won't linger. That more or less answers question three as well. Num-ber four, I'd imagine that you don't have to be in love to write that stuff, just key into the program and you're on. You've got your own answer to question six."

"You've missed out number seven."

Rainbow Hair hesitated. "Because I'm having trouble with that one myself."

Though the chocolate juices were still only a distant promise, Mog's stomach contracted. In the context of a library, a man with a multicolored coiffure and a list headed LOVE, SOME THOUGHTS AND QUERIES, the sensation was unique.

"I've also omitted question five," he said, leaning forward and tapping the page. The finger was

. . . long and efficient . . .

(for tapping paper, anyway) but she would not have described the nails as

. . . professionally manicured without a hint of effeminacy . . .

You had to be realistic.

"Of course, in that kind of book," Rainbow Hair was saying, "before the heroine will nip late at night with a suitor into a park—in her case, it would be his estate—all the bells have to be ringing. And I gather that with Denis she did not get a full peal." He stopped, his face sobered. "Christ! I shouldn't have mentioned that."

"Feel free." Mog smiled, aiming for "grimly," and failed.

"He took it badly. Seems to think he had got it made."

"*Him?*"

Rainbow Hair grinned. "Admittedly he's short of the ideal, but who isn't?"

"You sound as if you've undertaken to put in a word."

"No; he can look after himself. And he's not so easily put off."

"Is that a warning?"

"Only if you need it. It's more an assurance that Denis is an optimistic sort of bloke. Like me."

Mog looked down at her notes and began to embellish the title. She felt ill at ease because she could not be sure of his intention. Not that she would die a thousand deaths if she did not understand his meaning, but on an intellectual level she would like to get it right. Meanwhile, on a more mundane level, her stomach was registering a seismic disturbance. If this went on, she would have to cut out Mars bars as well as cigarettes. You could grow into a hypochondriac worrying about your health.

"Well, that seems to have put an end to our talk," Rainbow Hair said. "A pity you can't manage more. It belies your reputation. Why, I ask myself, am I the one singled out for short measure? It is an ironic choice since talk is my occupation at present; voluntary, of course. I put it on all the application forms: Interest, talk. Amateur, but going professional. Don't gnaw your nails, Mog; it's bad for your teeth. Then at last I recall the reason. Under number six you write that you have renounced our fair sex. Looking around, I can understand that, but it's a shame if you can't make the occasional exception. And this is no plea for Denis. I am deciphering it correctly, aren't I?" He rose, walked around the table, and stood behind her. "Yes. And it looks worse, the right way up. Very uncompromising." He was stretching over her, running his finger down the page. An earring dangled against her cheek. "You know, a second read suggests that a good deal of this is concerned with something more interesting than pulp romance. The heroine is never troubled by these sorts of riddles." He paused. "I shouldn't be looking at this. I'm sorry." The amusement had left his voice.

"It's nothing. I was talking to myself," wondering why she felt miserable and had apologized when he was in the wrong.

"No need to talk to yourself when I'm here. You could

pretend I'm an Agony Auntie and not one of the other half you have sacked."

His hand smoothing her collar was so light she could have been making it up.

"All right; I won't interrupt any longer, since it's talking to yourself you're after, Mavourneen. But don't despair. I'll be around."

Some comfort that is, Mog grumbled as he left the library. Though to be fair he had taken the questions seriously; he had been interested. Sometimes, when he was not being facetious you had the feeling that he could be on your wavelength. If you bothered to tune in.

Mog licked up the crumbs of chocolate stuck to the wrapper. Considering that a Mars bar was the centerpiece of Mr. Dab's hourly snack, it was astonishing that she had not been put off them for life, but she had determined not to be influenced. As she had once told him, he could have made a fortune advertising the product; he had certainly spent one eating it.

> . . . His hand came roughly down on her shoulder. For a
> moment a shudder, as of an electric current, ran through
> her . . .

She did not know why he had fiddled with her collar. Perhaps he suffered from ticks. Sent bananas by our Glenda's library books.

Catching up with your reading matter, he had said. And that behaving like Jane Eyre was emphatically no go.

He had sympathized with the difficulties. But that did not help her with the book.

The only thing to do was to stop worrying and begin chapter four. She had been mulling over the position for three weeks and all she had achieved was a list of seven questions. Now, rereading them, she wondered whether she had contracted softening of the brain. With Great-aunt Edith and her dad about, there was always that danger.

It was lucky she had other matters to attend to, Mog consoled herself as she walked down the corridor toward the next class. After the last half hour a spot of madness in *King Lear* would come as a relief.

That, however, did not reach her. At the door of the classroom was standing the flustered woman who had inspired the opening of the day nursery. "I'm waiting for Miss Simmons, to apologize for not coming into the class," she explained. "The rota has broken down and there's no one to look after the kiddies. I shouldn't complain, since it is very good of Mr. Beadle to let us have one. You suggested it, didn't you? I can't tell you how grateful we all are. It's made such a difference. But I was so looking forward to today's lesson. We never read any Shakespeare at my school," she apologized, blushing.

By the way Shakespeare was taught in most schools, Mog concluded from a sample of one, the woman was fortunate; but postponing description of educational techniques, she asked how the nursery was organized. Apparently there were about "ten of us" who shared supervision, leaping between classes and children. To Mog's remark that getting out of the house and into the school did not appear to be much of a swap, the woman answered with vigorous denial: to look after the kiddies in between whiles was a small price to pay for attending courses that were all out of this world.

Mog thought her evaluation excessive, but this was not the moment to implant a more balanced view. "I'll do it," she said and, without waiting for the predictable outbreak of gratitude, went.

"You're late," the previous keeper rebuked her, and fled.

Inside the room, Mog faced the assorted inmates. Apart from one cooling off in a pram, they relinquished their activities and stared. There followed a period of mutual assessment during which Mog reviewed her experience of children and discovered that it was nil. Of course, she had witnessed Ben's infancy but at the time, regarding it as totally unwarranted, she had stayed out of his way. However, a memory tapped at the sight of a thickset child, male, who was pounding the sand tray, and she made a quick note to keep upwind.

The rest closed in. Mog was inspected. For one, at least, she failed to come up to scratch. "Where's Mummy?" the girl demanded.

"In her lesson."

Clearly this was not good enough. The girl immediately opened her mouth and began a dismal keen. This had a flushing effect on her sinuses because two translucent worms appeared, slid down, and joined forces on her lip; the effluence was then recycled with a flick of her tongue. Undoused by the spray, her howls continued and two others with groupie ambitions added a descant of syncopated notes. This provided cover for a thin boy to investigate the contents of Mog's bag, but catching his sleeve in the zip and fearing that he had seen the last of his hand, he drummed his heels on the floor and emitted a terrified squawk. Deafened, the others halted.

"You are a miserable lot," Mog told them, unhooking the boy. "And don't you start again," she said to the keening one who was warming up for another bout.

She could see they were an undisciplined bunch, however, because this order was ignored in favor of a repeat; but before they had reached the climax a baby crawled through their legs and catching sight of Mog's tennis shoes, homed in with a toothless jaw. Watching, the rest turned down the volume while, to assist a healthy chew, one unfastened the laces and stuffed them in the crawling one's mouth. Mog was disinclined to commend the girl's initiative. She needed watching.

"What's your name?" she asked.

The question was not welcomed. The child's glare accused

Mog of impertinence. "Suzy," she at last confessed with disgust.

In a group of seven, Mog told herself, you can expect that one will be unfriendly; you can bet statistics will show a percentage impervious to natural charm. Of that, Suzy possessed little herself. She was a pallid child who looked at the world with resentment, continually pushing her dress into a small pair of trousers. Mog wondered whether her wearing them had any connection with the fact that the thin boy had lost his.

"My name's Mog."

You would not have thought there was anything funny in that, but according to current ratings it was the laugh of the year. Mog smiled tolerantly. Until Suzy, growing tired of comedy, delivered a show-stopping punch to the thin boy's head.

It took some time to quell the riot. As yet unlearned in team organization, they took to the floor and gave a demonstration of pile combat, notable for its rotary movement as the one at the bottom emerges and climbs to the top. Musical accompaniment was provided by weeping and wailing and the gnashing of teeth.

When they were quiet again, clothes straightened, limbs checked for damage, and all passed as fit, Mog suggested they went back to play. She needed a rest. A quarter of an hour with this mob took years off your life. Her proposal met with no enthusiasm and looking around, Mog could appreciate why.

They were in the room that housed the writing class during the evening, the school junk replaced by the kind thought suitable for children. And that was not much: a few soft toys, a heap of greasy blocks, some crayons, a knob or two of what might have been Play-Doh in its prime, a rubber boat beached beside a potty, and a number of mechanical artifacts dismantled or suffering from plastic fatigue. There was also a sand tray, resembling those supplied for cats—Mog hoped there had been no confusion—but it had been commandeered by the sturdy boy who was emptying it methodically with a miniature truck and a spoon. Mr. Beadle had not overdone provision. It was a case of economy taken to excess.

"We'll make things. You fetch the Play-Doh." She pointed to the thin boy. They gathered around.

Now, plasticine sculpture is a neglected art, Mog informed them, so the opportunities are wide open; but she advised them to choose something simple to begin with. They would all do a funny face that would fit on a thumb. The response was disappointing. They settled down to fashioning spheres and rolling out worms. Regretting their orthodox approach but still game, Mog relinquished art for mass production, began a flow-line system, and assembled the bits.

The finished constructs were greatly appreciated, though their life span was short. You had to be tougher than dehydrated plasticine to survive examination, squabbling, nails and teeth. But one piece was especially successful. Rescued by the second groupie, it was broken up, kneaded, and suffered a remold while she, rocking on her bottom and flushed with delight, looked on the verge of freaking out. Mog smiled at her. Thus encouraged, the girl enunciated a determined "Wee." You can go so wrong in interpreting behavior.

Mog pointed out that groupie two ought to know that was not the right moment to ask, but the girl refused to be dissuaded. Noting that her condition was arousing interest, Mog recognized the risk of infection. Frantically she appealed to reason, arguing that she could not take one off to the lavatory and leave the rest without a guard.

Then the keening one said, "My mum brought the pot."

During the next twenty minutes Mog discovered that children have an unrelenting grasp on fundamentals. Show them a pink chamber pot, available by the mile at your local pharmacist, and they will provide for its use. And when the contents have reached an optimum level they will wait while you dash around looking for a means of disposal, which is the Elizabethan method, through window with a brisk fling. Then they will start again. Also, you can be sure that, when motivation flags or resources are low, one of their number will weigh in with advice, i.e., the boy at the sand tray. Suspecting that the keening one was losing interest, he parked his truck and maneuvered himself into position.

"Right," he shouted. "Ten, eight, nine, three, four, six, now . . . FIRE."

The breakthrough did not occur until mothers arrived to collect.

Among the first was a stand-in, presumably a father. A dough-faced man with an emaciated mustache, he sidled through the door. Claiming the thin boy was a more lengthy procedure than he expected and by the time the trousers were returned they had taken a good battering; though held down by her mother, Suzy put up a tearing fight.

While at the ringside he confided to Mog, "I'm only here to fetch the missus and the kid. Thought I'd stretch my legs. The TV's like something I'm aunt to, this time of day."

If he is at home, probably unemployed, what's stopping him from looking after his son? Mog asked herself. Rephrasing it slightly, she repeated the question.

"He's better off here," the man answered evasively.

"Well, he hasn't got much, has he?" She gestured around. "What they need are easels and paints and clay instead of plasticine, and books and dressing-up clothes and things they can play about on, like a climbing frame and slide."

"I can see you're one with ideas," he said, grinning, and the look he gave her was not entirely limited to compliment on her imagination. "You one of the teachers?" he asked, leaning close.

For the first time it occurred to Mog that some men might

be switched on by intellect. This opened up a whole new area for contemplation and suggested that there might well be aspects of the male psyche that she had not yet thoroughly investigated. In fact, in the interests of scholarship and the book, she might have to undertake more research.

"Teachers are different from the way they was when I was a lad," the thin boy's father was saying wistfully.

"That's right." She halted, sensing a possibility.

. . . Then a shiver passed through her slight but exquisitely formed body etc. It was frightening, unexpected, but she knew at that moment that an idea, like a child, had been born . . .

"We like to keep open lines with parents, especially fathers. Do you know if there are any with time on their hands who might knock together some equipment for these kids?"

Men are a lethargic lot, Mog reminded herself as she waited; they will take ages to weigh up the most simple proposal. You never receive an immediate answer if it might commit them to some work. They will stand there, munching their nails or their lip, as if speech had gone out of fashion.

"I don't mind having a go," he said at last.

She was careful to express delight.

Moving into the corridor, they arranged to meet the next day. There were designs to consider, measurements to take, materials to order. Also, though she did not mention this, it was desirable that he acquaint himself with the children and she could guarantee a truly intimate knowledge after he had been into the day nursery and done a stint. That was an idea that could be developed, but before she had progressed far with it, Hard Man Sugden was approaching, his demeanor that of a janitor under stress. At five feet his aura had a lavatorial fragrance; obscenities and threats of vengeance could be heard issuing from his lips.

Mog thought it diplomatic to scarper.

SIX

The gap between her curtains let in the light but Mog kept her eyes closed. She had a strict attitude to sleep. It was one of the boring chores in life she would prefer to avoid, but once reconciled to the necessity she allowed herself a generous dose.

Turning, she felt a gritty substance on her pillow and though her alarm clock had not yet sounded, she opened her eyes. Her bed was covered with a white powder; other topographical interest was provided by small outcrops of rock camouflaged with green emulsion and snippets of felty dust. She looked up. Considering the mess, the hole in the ceiling, bordered by splintered laths and dripping antiquated cobwebs, was small. As holes go you might say it was unexceptional, but it had one unusual feature. At its center it held her father's eye.

Mog regarded this, wondering what would be the effect if Cyril had a squint.

"Sorry to wake you, Maggie," his voice apologized.

"Think nothing of it, Dad. It's nearly time for the alarm."

"I've had a little mishap," he informed her.

Mog decided there was no answer to that.

"While I was up here having a look," he explained. "You see, I'm thinking of opening up the loft."

"Dad, when people talk about opening up the loft they do not mean through the bedroom ceiling."

This intelligence caused a shock because there was a thud, noises of scrambling, and the eye disappeared, to be followed immediately by three fingers. These waved about, as if searching for their mates.

Suppressing the desire to climb onto her bed and give them a hefty tug, Mog shook the plaster out of her hair and got up. One affliction that Dona had escaped was a father (and mother, for that matter); in most of the books the heroine's parents were irrevocably dead. In life it was different; parent mortality was lower. Despite forty years of mishaps, her father had managed to hang on. And he could not even fulfill the requirements for the other men in the stories: managing a shop did not make him the head of an international business empire, for example, Dermot and Daughter Inc., and his latest idea hardly qualified him as an architect, especially in view of his success in his first job.

The hero of *An Anatomy of Passion,* however, could be relied upon. By chapter four he was already a young doctor of Nobel prize-winning material. Compared with him, the heroine remained unsatisfactory, but Mog had the feeling that she would soon improve, that the book was about to take off again, that something would turn up. Odd, how on certain days she had this conviction that things would go right.

More plaster fell as the ceiling bulged around the hole. "Don't worry your head about it," her father shouted. "Everything is going to be okay."

Mog sighed and dug her jeans from under the secondary fallout. It was amazing how he could be so certain, in spite of his unhappy record. She wondered whether she had contracted the trait.

One member of the family had escaped this congenital optimism: Fred. He was sitting at the bottom of the stairs and looking despondent. Perhaps he was suffering from agoraphobia.

"I'm not sure that dogs get it," Grace said. "He knows it's his day for the shed."

"That's not fair, every time Aunt Edith comes! This is his home."

"There's nothing I can do about that. Dying of rabies is one of her fads."

The threat of G. Aunt Edith was another reason for leaving home early; the first was the appointment with the thin boy's father. After cutting down breakfast to fruit juice, a bowl of porridge, and a mixed grill, Mog was ready to depart.

"She's here!" Grace interpreted as at the front door a massed choir tinkled, "We'll keep a welcome in the hillside; we'll keep a welcome in the vales."

As Mog opened the back door, the extension chimes, instead of repeating the tune at the front, clicked, buzzed, then scratched out, "Will ye no come back again?" Sometimes her father's incompetence had a touch of genius.

Determined not to miss the thin boy's father, Mog reached the college before the main rush. A punch-drunk typewriter could be heard from Myrtle's office, but the cafeteria was empty except for a man. His position at the table reserved for lecturers indicated his status; his premature arrival, the untarnished enthusiasm of one still fresh to the job. But now this alone did not sustain him. His head was lowered in an attitude of silent prayer. Since his plate held a scone bearing a faint insignia reminiscent of Noreen's thumb, Mog thought the precaution sensible.

"You'd be better off with the packet biscuits," she told him as he began a tentative bite.

The advice weakened his purpose. He replaced the scone hurriedly.

. . . Then he raised his eyes to hers and there was a wealth of meaning in his look . . .

The most probable reason for this was that he had been a master at the school she had just vacated. She must have started a fashion. He had been denied the excitements of teaching her, but she had made good his loss in a few minor ways. For example, she recalled an occasion when she had given at least fifteen minutes to a helpful analysis of his choice of dress. This, she noted, had undergone a slight alteration, no doubt thought appropriate for Nathaniel Chubb, but a pair of ill-fitting denims did not compensate for the rest of the three-piece suit. Not wishing to discourage this hint of experiment, Mog postponed criticism.

"You can scarcely make out the teeth marks," she said, examining the scone. "So why don't you change it for a bar of chocolate? Noreen wouldn't mind. It's the other troll that goes hysterical if you try to swap."

This was the sort of information essential to staff in the first months, preventing embarrassing blunders and making them feel at home in their new environment. Mog added several other useful cautions: Never park in the space reserved for the Principal; never tangle with the caretaker; avoid Myrtle at the end of the month because she suffers from P.M.T.

Colin Banks listened attentively but the effort to memorize this list was painful. His eyelids twitched.

"Thanks." Abstractedly, he dunked his scone in his tea.

Mog thought she might have overstated the pitfalls. "You mustn't conclude this place is nothing but a hotbed of problems. If you push yourself, you could find some fun even in the staff room. And there are always the extracurricular activities."

"Don't tell me," he pleaded.

"I mean, you can join any of the outings. They run quite a few. And that means a coach."

The significance of this detail passed unnoticed. He was stirring his scone-enriched tea and looking like Fred. More description was necessary. You had to make allowances for limited imagination.

"Last year the staff had a weekend in Paris," she began, adapting fact to the needs of her audience.

". . . They passed along the leaf-shaded boulevards in a sumptuously upholstered coach, their hair tossed lightly by the refreshing draft of the elegant ventilators, cunningly disguised as plump puckish cupids. All around them, Paris like a beautiful woman whom age cannot wither or custom stale her Palace of Varieties put on her silks and jewels and opened her arms to greet them . . ."

Mog paused. The attempted seduction of the heroine was six chapters off yet, but the form this had to take was too predictable. Boring. As well as the problems of LOVE, SOME THOUGHTS AND QUERIES, this was another reason why the book had run aground. Perhaps if she could make Josie less wet . . .

(. . . Then she knew that an idea, like a child, etc. . . .)

Mog grinned. Thinking quickly, she continued,

". . . And as the magic of the bewitching city entered their veins, he felt her fingers close over his hand, her thumb stroke the love line in his palm, and finding the crisp Savile Row linen over his knee, it began to move delicately, tactfully, upward, ever upward, unerringly toward . . ."

She became aware that Colin Banks wished to make a contribution.

"Look, I'm not on the staff here, thank God! I dropped in to see if I could join the wine-making class," and without thanking her for the information that he could buy a pack for that in Boots, he rose, hitched up his denims, and shambled off.

All right, so I made a mistake; there is no reason to get excited about it, she mouthed to his back. But there was plenty of reason for her own excitement. Colin Banks had been a catalyst. From now on the heroine would have more character, more interest. The sort you would like to meet in any book.

"I like it. I like it," Mog drooled to herself.

"You're looking more cheerful today," the thin boy's father greeted. "Look, I've fetched my mate. He's Walt."

It was a constructive meeting though at first promising only grade C because of the conduct of the thin boy's father. While grooming his mustache he stared at her, testing his capacity for X-ray vision by which he hoped to penetrate a couple of layers of cloth.

Walt was more practical. "It's the surface of the slide that might be a hindrance. We'll as like as not be having to cover it. Pete, any thoughts?"

Pete nodded, but chose not to disclose them. "What's your class?" he asked Mog. "I might drop in."

"What's your budget?" Walt asked.

Trust a man to interpolate that kind of niggling question. They do it for effect. They say it with a shrewd puckering of the eyelids and in a tone to imply that they would be Chancellor of the Exchequer—if they only had the Maths.

"The fiscal policy of the school is based on the Micawber system," she answered. Today looked like being fun. "Which is better than double entry since it records market fluctuations and is sensitive to the current value of stocks. That means that at all times the cash flow is fluent."

Walt nodded sagely. Pete ogled. Mog took another breath.

"It's smashing, you doing this for the children. It's fantastic.

I expect you'll need to spend some time with them, getting the right measurements, seeing what the kids are like. I'll arrange that for you."

"I know what kids are like," Walt told her. "I've three of my own and there are sixty in our street. We can get the measurements out of a catalogue." From which Mog deduced that he was reluctant to visit the nursery.

This was not quite good enough. If he imagined his duties stopped at making a slide, a playpen, a climbing frame, and a few easels, he was mistaken. Her new-look heroine would not let them off with that. *She* would see that they took their place on the rota. It was time the fathers got in where the action was. There was no blood to date, but she could vouch for the tears and sweat.

"You're not telling me you're put off by a clutch of under-fives!" she exclaimed, laughing. This was a crucial moment, the lighthearted preface to final persuasion. However, sensing that a hand on Pete's knee (definitely not encased in Savile Row linen) might be misunderstood, Mog put her elbows on the table, rested her chin in her hands and looked solemnly into his face. "They are a smashing little lot and very obedient. Enjoy a bit of a singsong and the occasional pee, but no trouble. When you've got them occupied on a climbing frame and whizzing down the slide, you'll not know they are there. The school is beginning an experiment to see how children relate to fathers and I should like you two to be the first to take part."

"It's your idea?" Pete asked, enthralled.

"That's right." And you could not be more truthful than that. "The best arrangement would be for me to put you down for a particular morning," taking out her notebook. "Which one do you prefer?"

"Hang on," Walt interrupted.

"The one you're in," Pete answered.

"We'll make it Monday, then. I'll get the list pinned up."

"Pete, it's not right, looking after a bunch of bloody babies," Walt alliterated with fervor.

"It's her experiment, Walt; scientific progress."

"Be buggered to that! What tale are we going to tell the lads in the Fighting Cock?"

"Depends how we tell it," Pete answered, grinning at Mog and treating her to what he intended to be a significant look.

Mog simpered, then on an afterthought squeezed out a wink. There are times when you have to make concessions. Put it another way, Pete's attentions were not entirely distasteful, though she assured herself that it was his cooperation and inclusion of Walt that finally scored the meeting an alpha plus.

It had, however, revealed a few minor difficulties such as covering the price of materials and reorganizing warders for the nursery. Neither of these was insurmountable, but it was Mr. Beadle's job to sort them out. Though it was unethical to adopt one of Dab's principles, there was much to be said for the delegation of tasks.

In her office, Mr. Beadle's nuts-and-bolts woman expressed her usual reluctance to disturb her boss. "He's busy."

That was more than could ever be claimed for Mr. Dab. "Good," Mog approved.

The answer provoked violent reprisals; Myrtle jabbed at the keys of her typewriter and gave the space bar a stunning punch.

"I think he'll be willing to see me," Mog said, and knocked on his door. As Mr. Beadle chimed a welcome, Myrtle delivered more blows to the typewriter; one of its occupational hazards was obviously a premature death.

At the sight of Mog, the Principal expressed a hesitant felicity and took cover behind his desk. The ring of confidence around his smile dimmed and he looked embarrassed, presumably because once again he failed to recall her name. Mog had read that such lapses of memory could be interpreted as an unconscious desire to forget, but she saw no reason why he should wish to do that.

"There are ways of remembering," she tried to be helpful. "You could think of it as part of a word, like transMOGrify. I like that. Or rhyming with another, like flOG or tOGgle. Or as an acronym for something, like Move Over Grandpa."

Mr. Beadle showed no immediate understanding. Mog sighed. He must be slow-witted.

"But of course!" The smile came on again. "It's Margaret Dermot."

"Mog, generally." Some people are irredeemably thick.

Deciding to waste no more time on memory training, Mog gave a brief synopsis of nursery developments to date.

"It is very good of them to volunteer to make equipment, but in my position one learns to identify needs, and I am afraid that there is no money available." Mr. Beadle shook his head gleefully and went through the pinch-eyed shrewd financier routine. "And I am not sure I can approve of fathers helping with supervision. I admire their willingness to do that, but in accepting their offer I may upset certain . . . interests. The school could find itself in very deep water, Floggle; it might be considered—how do you young people express it?—rather way out."

For a man with vision, this was disappointing. Mog frowned at his left earlobe while she considered her next move.

There was no need to request an explanation of the certain . . . interests. By which he meant attitudes. His. Babies were women's business, either at home or in the nursery. To have men involved would be the beginning of the rot. His own wife might even dump theirs in his office while she put up her feet and had a cigarette. But he had another interest. The school. Her concentration interrupted by the man's frantic pulling at the scrutinized auricle, Mog went into attack.

Later she had to admit to herself that without the practice

on Mr. Dab she might not have succeeded. It was odd how that man had provided hidden benefits. On the other hand, Mr. Beadle was not such a tough opponent, because he had a weakness. Ambition. You could not accuse Mr. Dab of that.

By the time she had finished, the Principal was exhibiting symptoms of rapture and he was eager to confirm everything she said. Indeed, he went further as he prophesied that the school would lead the nation, initiating new concepts in shared parenthood as men ran the nursery. This would be the axis for a course on Fathers at Risk, boldly tackling the problems of redundancy by offering training for a new type of job more imaginative than anything devised by the Manpower Services Commission and which would include associated crafts such as carpentry, to be developed in the school workshops with all the resources at their command.

As breath ran out, Mr. Beadle managed a final sentence: "I have to thank you, Tog, for bringing this to my attention."

"It was simply a question of identifying a need."

"I'll do a mail shot to all the fathers. People in this town hold traditional attitudes but I do not anticipate many refusals. They will cooperate." He smiled. "There are ways and means."

Mog walked down the corridor elated. Mr. Beadle needed a woman to straighten him out. One with ideas; one that could make the place hum. He was fortunate in having one available. And that little meeting had proved a satisfactory dummy run for the next chapters.

In chapter four the heroine, transformed, would relinquish her typewriter, take several degrees including a Ph.D., and be appointed principal of a revolutionary educational establishment over the head of a famous male contender. He, beguiled by her intelligence and good looks, would struggle for her attention, slog (also jog?) hard, in the hope of gaining a condescending compliment, and at all times strive to be attractive and fit, conserving himself for her. This would demand some manipulation of previous character and background, but she had never gone over the top about the surgeon hero and adjustment was easy. The advantage of this sort of book was that you could change the hero from a racehorse owner to an underwater filmmaker, or from a famous portrait painter to an Olympic runner, or from an eminent surgeon to a bungling lecturer in a school, and there was no difference.

"Morning," Rainbow Hair greeted, startling her, at her elbow. "Risk angina, trying to catch you up. Like a cup of coffee?"

She looked at her watch. "It's *Paradise Lost* in ten minutes."

"I can believe you. It never lasts long."

At the table he told her she was looking more cheerful. "That suits you. Do I take it that the problem is cracked?"

"Sort of. I'm altering the heroine drastically."

"I hope you don't overdo it. I liked her, in a mess. Except that she had given up men. Correction; I'm confusing. That was you, wasn't it? You can't have a woman in a love story doing that." He was laughing at her.

"I might have a go."

"It wouldn't get you very far. What's the alternative? Another woman? Wow! Not that I'm prejudiced, of course. I'm all for self-expression," stroking his hair, "but you can't blame us men for looking after our own interests. Being less personal, I must say the lesbian idea is very daring. It would be a unique contribution to pulp romance. An original statement, punching the convention under the belt. And if you're having second thoughts about it, I wouldn't; I mean, about putting yourself in a book. It's bound to happen no matter how you attempt to disguise it, so you might just as well relax and let it all hang out. Stop scratching your cuticles, Mog; you'll fetch blood. In any case, not many people will assume you are like that. I'd never have guessed if I hadn't had that clue about giving up men."

"I think you're foul," Mog said through her teeth.

"I improve on acquaintance."

It is impossible to give him the elbow, Mog raged to herself. You would have thought that to call him foul would be strong enough. Next time she would have to clarify with: vile, rotten, putrescent, lousy, pestiferous, unsavory, the pits. Contagious. Trying to ignore the last, any girl can make a slip, she pushed aside her cup and reached for her bag.

"I expect you are about to tell me I won't have the chance," he was saying. "Not today anyway. Soon you have to wrestle with Milton and I have to toil through the Situations Vacant; being unemployed is a full-time job." He rose. "But I have had time to meditate upon that list of yours, especially the last question. Difficult. In the end, I decided I should have to delay answer until I had the complete scenario to go on, but I'm working on it. I'll keep you informed." He bent over her and drew the backs of his fingers down her cheek. "Come on, refloat your sense of humor, Mog, and give it a whirl."

How can I when I don't know if he is joking? And why does he always go first? she asked herself, watching him squeeze round the tables. So that you should watch him, she answered, averting her eyes; also, in order that he can avoid explaining what he means. In that respect he could learn a lesson from Keith. Plus another one, like keeping his hands at a distance, she added, rubbing the tingling skin. By now he had probably reached the door, but she was not looking back.

. . . From the first moment he had met her he had experienced this strange attraction. It was there in the very marrow of his bones and once again his breath stopped as his fingers itched to stroke the soft curve of her cheek and his gaze rested upon her fathomless gray eyes which sucked in every fiber of his being. They spared nothing, eyeing with amused condescension the tell-tale effeminacy of his patchwork hair and the two o'clock shadow which, nervously, he fingered, wishing that today of all days he had been more thorough with his three-blade, rotary-action, floating-head Philip's Close Shave. He knew this woman was dangerous, ruthless; she threatened his peace and his hard-won resolution to renounce her sex, and in her presence he felt naked like a guilty Adam without the fig leaf's scant codpiece. For a moment a shudder as of an electric current ran through him. Then with a desperate little cry, almost a moan, he fell forward in a surrendering swoon . . .

SEVEN

Mog went through her list of projects for the week.

1. Essay on *Paradise Lost*. (Including appendix not submitted, entitled: Sharing the Apple, Eve's first mistake.) Done.
2. Essay on *King Lear*. Half done.
3. To do. Check Economic notes. (Don't trust the guff Anderson dishes out. Any man who holds up his socks with garters must be suspect.)
4. Obtain a poster.

This looked quite well over the patch in the ceiling. After suffering Cyril's Plastering for Beginners, she had discouraged his ambition to score with emulsion paint, saying that she would rather make do with a poster removed from the cafeteria bulletin board: DONATE A LIVER. Someone had added, "and claim a free helping of fried onions."

5. Check price of home computers.

By the side of the last item Mog wrote £130–£1,000, but she had already decided to buy at the cheaper end of the market; it was doubtful that the advance on the novel would stretch to everything. When she began to receive royalties and public lending right payments, she could offload this computer on

Ben and replace it with a more sophisticated model plus all the attendant software.

There was, unfortunately, a slight frustration.

It was now five weeks since she had sent the first three chapters to Cupid Books, but apart from a formal acknowledgment their response had been unsatisfactory. In fact, nil. She was puzzled by this since anyone would have been hard put to spend longer than twenty minutes reading what she had submitted; ten, for a slick reader. Perhaps they had some drudge committing it to memory before they returned the script, which would be a blatant infringement of copyright but difficult to prove. There was also the possibility that it was not usual to send out novels piecemeal with the request that the publisher should indicate whether he would be interested in the rest, whereas to her it seemed a sensible procedure. It could find you a market while still writing the book, so eliminating the time spent waiting after it was finished. An event as yet well out of sight.

The next two chapters had gone very smoothly. The heroine, transformed, had quickly silenced confusion set up by the Jane Eyre type; the hero, out of work now, was seeking to attract her attentions by dyeing his hair; and Nathaniel Chubb was providing convincing background detail and incidents. Admittedly the latter relied heavily on those originated by the author, but Nan Glen said it was always better to start with something you knew. However, in spite of this propitious development, again the output was slowing down.

Pencil in hand, Mog doodled, considering the reasons. Preparing for A levels was more work than she had imagined and a lot of leisure time had been taken up with tasks and distractions: supervising the nursery, conducting a market survey on Noreen's menus, restraining her father's do-it-yourself excesses, listening to Rainbow Hair. The last was becoming a habit but, whatever Josephine said, that did not prove she had gone back to men. He was addicted to the art of monologue, which made a change from Keith. In certain other tendencies there was an unhappy resemblance.

Mog sighed. It was very disappointing. Neither of those two gave a girl much to work on for the requirements of Cupid Books; which was the true reason why hers was in a decline. They provided no model for the tacky bits and by now these should be on the way. Of course, she could do them off the top of her head, but she might miss important detail. To be really professional it might be necessary to check—objectively. As she had said to Josephine, a writer sometimes has to make sacrifices in the cause of Art. The whole thing threw up a lot of issues. She would try to discuss them with Nan Glen.

"I thought you said that writing class might have to finish," Grace commented the following evening. "You've been going five weeks now, but there's no sign."

It was clear that the possibility of closure had been a sustaining hope.

"We still haven't a quorum but I put it to Mr. Beadle and he agreed that a school like his ought to have some creative content in its evening program."

"He must be as bad as the rest of them. I don't know what we are coming to when the head master of a place like that encourages that type."

"Mother, they are only people having a go at writing."

"Funny oddities, I bet."

"Does that include me?"

"You're my daughter, Maggie," attempting a decent loyalty. "I'm referring to the others; and I expect they're all long hair and patched jeans and smelly feet in sandals."

"You're a bit out of date. One wears a tulle hat."

Grace blenched. "Really, Maggie, I don't like to think of you in the company of people like that. He sounds perverted."

Mog decided against correction.

"Are you forced to have much to do with that one?" Grace whispered, and lurching to the cat door, offered her unfinished pork chop to the truncated Fred.

"Nobody *forces* you to do anything, Mother," she answered and watched Grace unreel scenes of Caligulan debauchery across her retina.

"Maggie, I wonder whether we did right in letting you go, but he was down his hole at the time. I can't get past that hat."

"There's no need to worry. It doesn't grab me at all. At the moment I'm more into hair sprouting through button holes," supplying an erotic detail for Grace to work on. With an imagination like hers, who needs a paperback Romance?

It was a sentiment Nan Glen might have approved.

Though details of school administration seemed beyond her grasp and she had a dilettante attitude to priorities such as coffee breaks, she conducted the class with a relentless efficiency reminiscent of the new-look heroine in *An Anatomy of Passion*. Everyone was expected to produce work for the delectation and comment of the rest. "If you come to a writing class, then you are damn well going to learn what it is to sweat," she was reported to have said to Denis, a mild sadism uncorked by the third whiskey. But, in the previous two hours before the alcohol content had been topped up, she was sympathetic and made no distinction among the motley collection of aspiration and talent.

This evening her principles were to be tested. Grimly egalitarian, she indicated that they were ready to listen, lit an untidy cigarette and began to roll another. It was Mrs. Kitson's turn to introduce her work.

Unlike the others, Mrs. Kitson did not exhibit symptoms of stress when required to do a public performance. There was no fingering of collar (man in the suit), no sudden dehydration of larynx (Mrs. Lewis), no intermittent scaling of nostrils (Denis). Indeed, Mrs. Kitson confessed to have anticipated the evening with great excitement, a feeling that appeared to have bypassed her fellows, and she had been so stimulated by its promise that the book had sprouted six chapters "almost by itself!" since they had first made its acquaintance. Unfortunately time prevented her reading them all, so she would just put the class in the picture and then give them a little taste of how it was coming on.

Adopting Mog's scenario, Mrs. Kitson had dragged her heroine round Morocco in the wake of her boss, who regarded her as a mere extension of his dictating machine and was oblivious to the latent fire smoldering beneath her shy exterior. One never-to-be-forgotten break in the daily routine had been a party to which she had been invited and where she had played charades. In one of these they had performed a wedding ceremony with heroine as bride and boss as groom. The irony of this had been so intense that even a nightcap of milky Ovaltine had failed to lull the heroine into untroubled slumber. Not long after this she was accosted on a street in Agadir, bundled into a taxi, blindfolded and driven away.

"I shall now *read on,*" Mrs. Kitson announced portentously.

"When she came to, Crystal looked round and saw to her astonishment that she was in the cabin of a yacht. She knew this because it resembled pictures she had seen on films and because there was a tiny porthole at her shoulder through which she could see waves gently skimming past and a sea gull hovering as if alert for its innocent prey. Tears of compassion started in Crystal's eyes at the thought, for was she not, too, like the herring, a victim of some remorseless power whose identity was a safely guarded secret?" Here Mrs. Kitson treated her audience to a pause, allowing them to appreciate the force of her comparison. "But that was not all. It suddenly occurred to Crystal that she was chained hand and foot to the narrow bunk."

"That'll teach her," Albert approved. Mrs. Kitson ignored him.

"Panic seized her and sheer terror froze the blood in her veins. She began to struggle, but to no avail. The bonds were new and every padlock was locked. Then before she was barely recovered from this terrible shock she heard the door of the cabin creak and a man entered." The pace of Mrs. Kitson's reading began to quicken. "He was dressed in a brilliant crimson gown stretching to the floor . . ."

"They call them djellabas," Denis corrected.

Undeflected, Mrs. Kitson said, "Do they really?" and continued, "The lower half of his face was hidden under a yashmak fringed with gold thread, leaving only his eyes that stared out, unfathomable and shrewd. Crystal wanted to cry out but she was overcome by a mysterious weakness as he stepped toward her and drew his fingers along the generous bow of her lips and dabbled them in the hollow of her throat. She knew she was alone in a ship's cabin with a man whose power oozed from the very tips of his fingers and, horrified by her predicament, she tried to rise but the chains held her down. 'Who are you?' she whispered, but he made no answer as he bent to untie the pretty ribbons at her neck." Mrs. Kitson had begun to pant. "His fingers were compelling but gentle and, despite herself, she felt her flesh surrender to his touch. She knew this was wrong and again tried to resist but she could not move and was as putty in his hands. Then, as the final ribbon on her blouse was pulled loose, a great surge as of a tidal wave passed through her. He bent over her, his hands searched and she found herself locked in his arms. Outside the porthole the sea gull dived for the innocent herring, but Crystal was floating on a great tide of ecstasy, her eyes closed, drifting as in a dream."

Exhausted, Mrs. Kitson laid down her papers, straightened her hat, and smiled winsomely at her audience. There was a noticeable reluctance to meet her eyes.

"I reckon he should've done her in," Albert judged, and began to sketch a shroud over a recumbent model.

Mrs. Kitson was appalled. "He wouldn't do that! She is his wife!"

"But you never told us she was married," Mrs. Lewis objected. "How can she be married when she is in Morocco and in love with her boss?"

"Because *he* is her husband," the other explained. "That is revealed later. You see, when they were playing charades it wasn't a make-believe wedding they had, but the real thing." Nan Glen drew noisily on her third cigarette, halving its length. "It's a way of keeping you in suspense," Mrs. Kitson continued. "You see, you think it's some Arab chieftain, but later you learn it's her boss who is now her husband, come to claim his own."

"His own?" Nan Glen managed through racking coughs.

"His wife," Mrs. Kitson reminded her. "So we know what happened was all right."

This assurance was not entirely persuasive and the suited man expressed a doubt concerning the chains.

"Oh, they just came to me out of the blue," she answered serenely.

It would have been better had they stayed there, appeared to be the majority opinion, though Albert nodded and clamped handcuffs to his subject's wrists.

"What's he doing messing about with them, since they're married? I mean, it's a bit late for the kinky stuff, isn't it?" Denis argued. "Okay, so you put all that in for kicks, and she obviously goes for it, but you can't stop there and not say what they get up to. I mean, how many people want to hear about herrings and gulls and surf riding when there's a couple having it off?"

Mrs. Kitson's lips thinned. The hat quivered with revulsion.

"You're no more nor less than a pervert. All you're interested in is mucky sex," she hissed.

Then, with the air of having just purged a rampant vice, she sought another more worthy of her attention. It fell upon Mrs. Lewis. "That's all men think about, isn't it?" she declared confidently. "But we women are different, aren't we? What we want is *love*, both to give and to receive; and whatever happens, we will find a way."

It was an optimistic premise and could have been a useful slogan for the world peace movement, but in the context of being chained to a bunk the likelihood of discovering a route to this ideal state seemed remote. This thought troubled Mrs. Lewis.

"I don't know if I'm the right one to ask," she stammered, greatly agitated. "I'm a very ordinary sort of person and I haven't thought much about it. It's just how you feel, isn't it? But I must say, if Mr. Lewis was ever to start on anything like that—which he wouldn't—I don't think I'd be able to enter into it, somehow. To tell you the truth, Mrs. Kitson, I wouldn't know which way to look!"

This was received in what verged upon hallowed silence, threatened only by signs of rallying from Mrs. Kitson. Before this could occur, Nan Glen took over.

Undoubtedly Mrs. Kitson would acknowledge the helpfulness of everyone's frank reaction, but it was, she felt, occasionally confused. Her own frank reaction was not so much confused as desperate and after ten minutes' struggle between objectivity and personal taste, Nan Glen gave up.

"I think we should benefit from a coffee break," she admitted, sagging in her chair. Mrs. Kitson's prose had created a precedent.

But as the room emptied, Nan Glen roused herself. "I'd like a word," she called to Mog. Then accusing, "I noticed you kept quiet. Having originated the idea, are you satisfied with the result?"

Harsh but, Mog had to admit, justified.

"I was only trying to help."

Nan Glen snorted.

Mog propped herself against a desk. Mental stress had sunk to her legs. The only other occurrence of this physiocerebral interaction had been the evening Keith had outlined a six-year plan ending in marriage and he had gone as far as sitting her down and pushing her head between her knees. This was an awkward position for anyone with amorous intentions to follow up, but Mog considered that a fellow with an ounce of initiative would have managed. Keith didn't. Tonight these symptoms were induced by Nan Glen's jaundiced glare.

"I don't think it was bad as a piece of satire," Mog tried.

"Satire! She believes in it totally," the other snapped. "Do you read romantic novels, then?"

"I've glanced at a few. I think they would be very easy to imitate," aware of the quicksands under her words.

"Perhaps; but that is not why we are here. Whatever you write, you try imitating something else, and it will show. You'll convince nobody." A missionary flush crept over Nan Glen's nicotine-raddled cheeks. "It's got to be from yourself, blood and guts."

"I don't see how that is always possible. I bet Mrs. Kitson has never been chained to a bunk."

Nan Glen's demeanor suggested that a double whiskey would not come amiss, but she contrived a weak smile. "Don't misunderstand me. It's a question of getting inside and then conveying a situation."

Mog considered that Mrs. Kitson had done that all right, but thought it best to keep quiet.

"I am concerned with the success of the passage in literary terms," the other continued. "Though I admit it is difficult to avoid personal prejudice. Frankly, I find the conventional sort of humping quite adequate to my needs."

They giggled and Mog discovered that her legs had recovered their usual strength.

"But to be fair, the chains, though hack, are still a pertinent metaphor. Woman is born free but everywhere she is in chains," Nan Glen mused. "It was a pity she could not have given the old formula writing a new look; and make the description more precise. That would be hard without more imagination; but lacking that, she could have employed an alternative. She could have gone out and done some field work."

"A sort of sacrifice in the cause of Art?"

"Whose sacrifice?"

It was some time before their laughter slackened, then, as if conscious that it was unethical to discuss another member of the class, Nan Glen attempted to compensate.

"You haven't produced anything yourself yet, Mog. I shall be interested to see some of your work."

Mog suffered another bout of no confidence in her legs. She did not think this was the most sympathetic atmosphere for introducing *An Anatomy of Passion*. It was just possible that the improved heroine would appeal, but there might then follow an interrogation on the origin/style/purpose/plot/attitudes/tone/structure/narrative method/background/quality of writer's thought/ditto descriptive powers—all that stuff.

"I've been rather busy lately," she answered.

"Haven't we all?"

Mog looked round, praying for a quick distraction. At home you could always rely on one: a loony remark from G. Aunt Edith; a frenzied scratching by Fred; a mishap by her father; an anxious squeak from Grace; a fart from Ben. Nothing presented itself except the nursery equipment stacked in a corner to make room for the writing class desks. Despite punishing use, some traces of varnish still glimmered on the slide and climbing frame, labors of love by Pete, labors of carpentry by Walt. Off duty, the plastic potty rested under an easel and a sloughed nappy provided a damp nest for crayons. In a follow-up to his six-year plan, Keith had fathered three babies.

"I've got some poetry," she said and, raking through the litter at the bottom of her haversack, she exhumed three of his poems.

"Good." Nan Glen stretched out a hand.

Mog scanned the poems hurriedly. Written in the first person, there was nothing in them, as far as she could remember, to betray the sex of the author. Which was not, in any case, an attribute he carried to excess.

"Hmm," Nan Glen murmured, her eyes on a first line.

As the scrutiny continued, Mog became aware that her solution might be ill-judged. Quick thinking in an emergency was all right, but it could land you in a bigger fix. Apprehensive, she began, "There's one little thing I ought to mention . . ." but was prevented by the return of the rest of the class.

"Fancy a drink?" Denis invited later.

Two months earlier Mog would have refused, but tonight she hesitated. Denis had certain . . . attractions that were difficult to ignore, particularly when he leaned close.

"Come on," he urged. "You always rush off."

"I wouldn't have thought you noticed. Aren't you generally occupied with Nan Glen?" The retort was straight out of one of our Glenda's library books and Mog was pleased with it. Had she known how to perform the action, she would have tossed her head.

"No need to be jealous," he said, preening himself at the thought. "She's biddable for a drink, but after that . . ."

Detailing the subsequent bids was unnecessary. He put a hand under Mog's elbow and steered her toward the Dray-man's Arms.

Just like a man to assume you are jealous, Mog thought, but had no time for correction. She was occupied with issues more urgent. One was how to reconcile her present company with the no-man diet she had maintained for so long. But she had begun to wonder whether she was doing herself a disservice by denying herself more thorough acquaintance with half the world's population (ignoring Rainbow Hair for the sake of argument). Without the occasional in-depth reminder of the unregenerate male a girl might believe that "God's in her heaven and all's right with the world."

It was for this reason that she had accompanied the present unregenerate male into the Drayman's Arms, Mog told herself firmly. And squashed against him at the bar, she added the necessary rider that her acquiescence was totally unconnected with the sensations he evoked.

"I'm under age," she pointed out as Denis signaled to the barman.

"What for?" he demanded predictably.

Mog sighed. It was lucky she had no excessive expectations about the intellectual quality of the evening. Nor about anything else, she added hastily.

At this hour the Drayman's Arms would have served as a handy model for Mr. Beadle's ambitions. One way or another it entered the life of every member of its catchment, founded on the unpretentious no-nonsense base of beer. As a result, it was packed out.

"Let's try the Snug," Denis said, nudging.

Mog wondered whether the name indicated only coziness and, following Denis, she compiled a few derivatives with more action: to snug, snugging, snugged, snugger, snuggable, snug making, snug match, snugsick, snug letter, snug story, snuglorn.

The last described most of the occupants. They were a depressing lot, for the most part occupied in silent requiem for sinking pints. Subordinate to this invigorating activity, the few women present toyed with insipid concoctions and laughed on demand. In between times, with eyes unfocused and expressions hopeful, it was possible that they had undergone temporary reincarnation as Dona or Crystal and, shrewdly pierced by ice-blue eyes (now thawing), were clamped by the iron biceps of a suntanned, infinitely experienced tycoon. Looking at the factual alternatives, Mog thought that even Nan Glen would sympathize.

Meanwhile the alternative on offer to her was demanding her full attention. Though he was in tune with the Snug's beer-quaffing dedication, that was not his priority. She was. With particular reference to the bits of her that came within his reach. These were waist, left shoulder, left hand, and a fair portion of the left thigh. The other thigh, wedged behind a table leg, was somewhat off the circuit, but nevertheless it received an occasional quick pat. Mog found the peripatetic nature of this investigation confusing since, not knowing where Denis would alight next, she was unable to prepare a repulse; also, it had a unique symptom. It reduced her powers of conversation to a mush.

Denis suffered no such disability. "You know, I wondered about you after that last time," he told her.

At that moment his arm was round her shoulder and his mouth close to her ear. Having no memory of a similar occasion, Mog floundered. Her answer was a weak, interrogative croak.

"When I was walking you home," he expanded.

The arm dropped twelve inches and squeezed. Mog assured herself that no one with compressed lungs could be expected to articulate.

"Like I said, the way you suddenly went off made me think. We were doing all right, weren't we? I mean, I was all for it and you were showing an interest. Then . . ." Denis cracked the thumb and second finger of his free hand. "There you were, gone!"

"I had work to do," Mog contrived to remind him.

"So you said." His dexterity was amazing. In some respects her father would benefit from his example. With one hand Denis could light a cigarette, striking the match against his thumbnail, or remove the crown cap from a bottle of Guinness and top up his beer, while with his other hand execute innumerable variations on the basic massage routine.

"Do you know, I've never had that before? I'm not saying I haven't been stood up; that can happen," he admitted magnanimously in a tone that conveyed the odd frustration was inevitable in a lifetime's experience. "But nobody's ever told me they didn't want it because they had to *work.*"

It did seem a perverse choice. Mog smiled and with her unyoked shoulder attempted a shrug to indicate that she shared his incredulity. "Short of time," she managed into her glass.

"Time!" Denis exclaimed. "I wasn't thinking of taking all night!"

This was an aspect of the procedure that Mog had not considered. She regarded the hand taking a deserved nap on her knee. In fact, there were many aspects she had not considered and if this went on much longer she reckoned there would be a good many more. Imagination had not been adequate. In this instance, would Nan Glen have recommended field work? The hand was long and bony. Surprising how, so narrow and thin, it could generate such heat. Pretending to measure, she stretched her own over it.

"So you'll appreciate," Denis concluded, "why I thought you were a tease."

Mog was revolted by the designation. "Just because I decided to go home!" she defended. It was not the moment to analyze motives, or to judge what had happened from his point of view. "It suits you, doesn't it, to say I was that; it's very convenient. Obviously it couldn't be any fault of yours that I didn't want to go into the park, could it? I have to be a tease, to let you off the hook!"

You would have thought that would settle him, but men are impervious to criticism. All he did was take a long rinsing drink, then open another button on his shirt and groom the pert hairs.

"You can't half pack a punch," he told her, grinning. "I guessed as much. And I'm not complaining. I mean, passivity just doesn't turn me on. You can do better watching TV. But there was no call to take me up like that. I was only speculating. I said I *thought* you were, afterward. I soon changed my mind. I decided you aren't."

He administered a quick peck to her cheek then sat back and smoothed his hair. Unstudied, the movement was deft and brisk; the hair fine, newly washed, and curved to his head. Though there was a distinct absence of sculptured good looks and Savile Row tailoring, he was, Mog groaned to herself, very visual. He was also at that moment without conceit or vanity. He was absorbed in her.

"And you know how I decided? Meeting you week after week at the class, I got the message. You're straight, Mog. You're too damned honest to be a tease."

At which Mog became as one of Mr. Beadle's hapless vessels, adrift. She tried to find anchorage by examining Denis's pronouncement, but whether it was sincere compliment or calculated did not seem relevant. He had played an ace. From now on she knew it would be impossible to draw back.

The trouble with me is, I've got these principles, Mog told herself as she and Denis abandoned the Snug. And worse, I have to live up to them, she added as their feet found tarmac, gravel, then an obsolescent path. It's a habit that one of these days will get me into a fix, wondering briefly whether this was one such day as they set up jangling oscillations along a line of children's swings. ("That's no good; not stable," from Denis.) Here I am, perched on a roundabout, proving I'm not what he said (her hands around his neck), and it's not as if I can leave it like that (her mouth finding his); I have to do it to excess. That may be a hereditary factor; it runs in the family, finding expression in many different ways (unfastening the final button of his shirt). Like my father's do-it-yourself mania, and G. Aunt Edith's aiming at the world title for her collection of dentures, and my mother freaking out every time she imagines (her bra going slack) me plus a man. Keith, of course, being the exception. (It was dark, but Denis was not only visual.) An exception in many respects when you thought of it. An anachronism, really. Which you might say gave him an irritating distinction. ("Come this way a bit, then we can lie back.")

There must be more comfortable things to lie on than a slatted, boxed-in roundabout with its center pole denting your head. Dona and Crystal would not have put up with it, legs hanging over the edge and heels pinned to the platform. They would have been treated to something more plush. On the other hand, when it came to essentials, they did seem to miss out. (Denis guiding her hand towards his zip.) They might have ecstasy in full spate and the innermost core of their being chugging on like it had gone bananas, but they were not keyed in to the action along the way. In fact, they were miserably short on technical detail.

And so was she, Mog admitted to herself (helping to sort out a tangle of knees and legs). Though Denis did not appear to be aware of it. ("You're quite something, Mog." "Umm.") He was, too; she had long ago stopped pretending to ignore his tactile attractions. But sensations were not entirely unqualified. There was an unpleasant urgency in the hand rubbing at her tights and she did not much like poking inside his zip. She was beginning to think that imagination might have advantages; at least it did not leave you high and dry with the facts.

Denis strove to gain a purchase on the ground with his feet. The roundabout moved. Momentarily off balance, he slid over her. His chest was warm, the hairs exciting.

So much for an in-depth reminder of the unregenerate male, Mog groaned. So much for not being a tease.

The roundabout continued to spin.

Then Denis said, "You're all right, aren't you?"

"I'm suffocating."

"I mean, you've seen to it?"

For a second, incredibly, she did not understand. Then, "No."

"Christ! And I've come without."

Gradually the roundabout slowed down.

"Feel like chancing it?"

"I'd rather not."

"Another time, then."

"Perhaps."

"You're nice, Mog."

"Thanks. So are you."

All his swagger had disappeared with its purpose. Standing by the roundabout he was only a shape, insubstantial.

"I'm sorry," Mog said. Surprised by the desire to cry. And wondered whether, in those last minutes, he too had been an exception.

EIGHT

"Like I told you weeks ago, Mog, you were bound to get over him."

"There was never anything of Keith to get over."

Josephine propped a mirror against the bottle of tomato ketchup, spat on the cake of mascara and kneaded in the brush. "In that case you could have been a bit quicker taking up with someone else."

"I haven't taken up with Denis."

"You've spent an hour or two with him in a pub. Knocking back the shandy. That's a start." Narration of events beyond the Snug had been omitted. "There'll be more to come, so don't fret. I mean, after being antimen for a couple of months you'll need some running-in time." Josephine cackled, approved her reflection, and began to thicken the lashes along a top lid. "Out of practice."

"I'm not sure I want to be into it."

"Depends who you are practicing with." Josephine liked that. "Knickers," she said, cutting short her appreciation. "That's made me smudge."

It was infuriating to see other people revved up when she was worn out; it was depressing. Mog could see no reason for the other's euphoria, but she tried to be patient. "You could be right about the practicing. That's not so far from what I've been thinking about all this last week."

Alert to the warning, Josephine looked at her watch and indicated that she had a typewriter booked in five minutes.

She ought to control this addiction to her typewriter, Mog told her. They would have robots and microchips going off their heads tapping away by the time she was on the market for a job. She would be wise to jack it in and aim for the executive level. That would be sound economics with, she might add, a philosophical bonus since she would be promoting sexual equality.

Concentrating on brushwork, Josephine was excused comment.

Mog pulled out her notebook, remarking upon this valuable side effect of the Dermot-Dab confrontations; to insure a true record of an argument's progress she had formed the habit of methodical tabulation of opinions, however crappy his were.

"Sometimes, Mog, I feel sorry for that man," Josephine said without moving her lips.

Deferring a caution against unnatural clemency, Mog flicked over her notes on possible men, purchases, and plots. Copyright for alliteration was not held by Walt. "It's sort of matters arising from your Glenda's library books, with some personal observations. Headed, MALE–FEMALE ENCOUNTERS."

"Well, it would be, wouldn't it? Have you mentioned the underwater encounters with the swimming instructor? That should be kinky enough. Oh, blast! Made a rubbish job of this eye. Have to start again."

If you want a sympathetic ear, nobble a friend, Mog reflected; and if you want a serious opinion, forget it. Josephine's behavior suggested that she had been investigating some new talent as yet not reported on but probably encountered at a disco last Saturday where, oddly enough, she had also met

Keith. He was always rushing home to pick up a blanket or saucepan or tons of his mum's ginger cake and Josephine had said she had had a long talk with him that, in view of his conversational blockage, must have been a strain. So there must be another man; you didn't get high like this on a shot of Keith.

"Just give me the general idea," Josephine added. Her tone implied that, for encouragement, the offer was hard to beat.

Mog looked at the pages, ruled into two columns: BOOKS and FACTS. There was nothing worth commenting on in the first paragraphs. For Dona and Crystal, ocean cruisers and sun-drenched beaches might have the edge on a children's playground behind the Drayman's Arms, but they were only the packaging; it was the goods that mattered. That caused the difficulty. Though it was not one that Mrs. Kitson's Crystal was aware of; despite constrictions of ironmongery, she simply freaked out. Whereas under FACT everything was less certain, including yourself. For example, she did not go a bomb on all that poking and pulling. (Her tights were like rags. She should not have thrown them into the washer; Grace had zoom-lens vision.) Nor did she much care for her thigh being pulverized by his knee. On the other hand, the business had its points; there was a lot to be said for it, Mog conceded. So much, she realized, scanning the next five paragraphs, that she doubted whether it ought to be said to Josephine.

She was waiting, her mascara brush poised. This attitude suggested she was reluctant to hazard a jab until she had got over the coming laugh. Without intention, Mog obliged.

"I suppose in the end," she said weakly, "it all boils down to sex."

That was better than Josephine had expected. "I'll never finish these; too much competition," she said at last, returning the brush to its case. "You mean to say it has taken you three pages to come to that conclusion?"

"It's how you do it, I'm talking about," Mog defended.

"Well, yuss," the other managed.

"In a book, I mean." Mog ground her molars. "Describing. It's got to sound right. Look, Jo, when a bloke's grabbed, have you ever floated on a great tide of ecstasy, your eyes closed, drifting as in a dream?"

It was some time before Josephine sobered up. "I wish you'd lay off, Mog. Why don't you try it out on somebody else?" Then, regarding herself in the mirror, she licked the tip of a finger, sleeked an eyebrow, and added, "Since you ask, I have to say no. But there's always hope." She giggled.

Mog wished that she could join her.

"And while we're on about it," Josephine added, "I'd advise you to cut out the dream bit. If it's going to be like that, then I reckon you want to stay awake for it, don't you?"

Mog decided this was not the moment to deny authorship of the lines. "Thanks for the tip."

"Any time," Josephine said, flattered.

"All right, what about this?" Mog referred to her notes in the column BOOKS. "When you go out with a man, Jo, do you want him to . . . well, take over? Do you feel that you want to be completely in his grip, like mastered?"

The other's mouth gaped. Eventually she was able to utter: "D'you *mind?* I wouldn't trust any of them an inch."

Mog sighed. "I'm not talking only about having it away."

"You could have fooled me. And I'm only saying, really. I easy might. It depends who it was. Or is," laughing again.

"I don't think I could, not the way this lot do," Mog persisted, tapping the pages. "They want him to be the boss all the time."

"Mog, I don't like to say this," Josephine said with relish, "but you are growing morbid."

Mog nodded.

"In addition, you are looking decidedly off."

If your confidence needs a boost, ask a friend. "Well, yuss. I think I must be reaching the midlife crisis."

"I'd say that's premature but it can be a relief. My mum doesn't mind because she can't get pregnant."

Mog thanked Josephine for reminding her of that compensation.

"Why don't you forget that book for a while and give yourself a rest?"

It would be nice, Mog thought, if

. . . her eyes were full of concern. Her complexion, all English peaches and cream, was unmarred by the artificialities of makeup, for on the wards she would wear nothing except the faintest hint of lavender scent. Her glowing, youthful health contrasted with the tired, sallow face of the patient as she bent over the bed, but strangely it was she whose hand trembled as she reached for the lean wrist and her fingers, though capable and sure, looked impossibly small as they searched for the weak pulse . . .

Instead, Josephine repeated her advice to stop worrying about the book. A handy replacement would be a man. She was not sure whether Denis was quite Mog's type, but he would do to be going on with. That was what she needed. With a boyfriend she would see everything differently. She would not waste her time agonizing on how these heroines behaved but get on with it herself. It was not natural, going around analyzing as she did. Doing it for school work and Dab was not unreasonable, but to extend the habit to men would only get her in a fix. Nobody was perfect. In fact, Mog objected to people that were, a prejudice well illustrated by her opinion of the saintly Keith.

This harangue, decorated with examples and digressions, took some time and left Mog picking at her cuticles and wondering from whom Josephine had learned such loquacity. Answer was prevented by the date with the typewriter. And who am I, Mog thought despondently, to compete with that? The day promised to score a D, probably minus (in brackets).

After this failure with Josephine, she questioned whether it was possible to gain rational consideration of her problems, but Rainbow Hair might try; she would have a go at him. Though it was unlikely that he would know if women liked being pinned down by a fella, being the passenger with him in the driving seat. The whole business was very hairy; indeed, with special reference to Denis (note the chest), it was practically hirsute. Mog sniggered. But Rainbow Hair might have an opinion about Crystal who went into a trance of passion (passion?) and left the technology to the man. A good example of traditional division of labor. There ought to be an alternative and she would have to research it, not for personal use, of course, but for *An Anatomy of Passion*.

Nor was she alone in this commitment to scholarship. As she gathered up her baggage Mog noticed two young men at the next table distinguished by their concentration on a book and, catching an exclamation, she listened in.

"Hey, Mike, look at this! She's got her legs around his neck!"

Mog squinted through the gap between the two bent heads and joined in examination of the sketch, reflecting that either the need for research was infectious or she was subject to a coincidence that might have squirted from the pen of Thomas Hardy. Mog was into him; this week she was crusading through *Tess*.

"I'd steer clear of that. Dangerous," Mike observed.

"You reckon? It says they favor it."

"I'm not talking about *her*. It's the bloke. All she has to do is bring her knees together sharpish and, crack." Mike demonstrated by thwacking the sides of his head with his palms. "Out for the count. You got to be realistic, Trev."

Interpreting this as a challenge, Trev suggested a practical solution. "You could wear your helmet."

"Look, I'm not joking. There's birds around that show no respect. I was down in Birmingham last weekend at my cousin's and we got talking with this bird in a pub and it turned out she went to Unarmed Combat. They have classes in it! So's they know what to do if they're mugged. She grabbed our Nige and showed. First they go for your eyes, then they sock you on the jaw, then they elbow you in the throat, and if you're still on your feet after that, they knee you in the goolies."

"But you're not supposed to be mugging them, Mike."

"I know that; but do *they?* Some of them are a bit short in the upper story. They can easy get the wrong impression. This fancy stuff is all right for some, Trev, but at the end of the day you have to look out for yourself. And this next one! They've got her on top! Now that's just asking for trouble. She's got it on a plate, hasn't she? No way could you defend yourself, stretched out like a nut on your back. She takes a sudden dislike, and you're done. 'Specially if she's one of this Unarmed Combat mob. Best stick to the usual, Trev. Safer."

Mog was enthralled. Mike's concern about preservation was surely a very modern dilemma. She doubted whether caveman had experienced such apprehension. On the other hand, cavewoman probably had. It would be no joke to try wielding a club from a supine position with your arms pinioned to your sides. She considered interrupting to point out that Mike's anxiety was a fair summary of the woman's situation but decided that he might not be receptive to the idea at that moment. Nevertheless his interest was encouraging and ought to be built on. She would draw it to Mr. Beadle's attention.

It is another unit we could add to the Environmental Studies, she rehearsed.

June Oldham

MR. BEADLE: *(The usual mumbles. Surreptitious glances at his watch)* . . . already covered in schools . . .

MOG: Barely, if you'll excuse the pun. I'm not talking about biology and fertilization but instruction on how to go about it. And, if you like, avoid it. I see it as a very practical course. In a college like this it is almost a growth industry.

MR. BEADLE: *(Embarrassed. Cough, cough)* . . . students well behaved . . . bookings for summer camp always full . . .

MOG: It is essential to the study of human behavior. Techniques employed would reveal many of the elementary, not to say elemental, assumptions of men about women. I think you should know that there are many students in the college already wrestling with the profundities of copulation. Such a unit, for anyone who has the courage to take up the challenge, is a superb opportunity to catch the imagination of the public and redirect the thinking of educational institutions up and down the country.

MR. BEADLE: *(Panting)* . . . Staffing problems . . .

MOG: I have just learned that it is to be introduced in a large college in Birmingham as a natural extension to their classes in Unarmed Combat. A pity if they got in first.

MR. BEADLE: I was merely voicing practical considerations. Even a man of vision is subject to those.

MOG: *(Rising)* Speaking of practical matters, there is one innovation in college facilities that would be an obvious adjunct to the course: a dispenser for male sheaths in the girls' lavatory. As a piece of equipment it would not be expensive to install; as a symbol, it neatly defines the creative tension between practicality and vision, the attribute for which Nathaniel Chubb is becoming increasingly renowned.

The last item she would definitely bring up. It would broaden the ethos of the school. Or, expressed another way, it might come in handy. As Josephine said, there is always hope.

But before making the suggestion, she had an hour of *Paradise Lost* and a visit to the day nursery. You would not have imagined there could be any similarities, Mog reflected later, but there was not much difference between the Milton/Adam insistence on female inferiority and what was going on in the nursery. Had Suzy given her mind to it, she would have agreed.

She was standing behind the door as Mog entered, glowering at her peers as, hands linked, they described a shuffling circle in the middle of the floor.

"She refuses to play. She's just dug her heels in, the little monkey. Nobody else is such a trouble." Suzy's mother blushed for her daughter's intransigence. "I'd take her around, only someone has to change his nappy," bouncing the pram tenant on her arm.

Choosing not to be that someone, Mog said, "I'll look after her."

"Now you go and skip around with Mog, else I don't know what that nice Mr. Gibson will think," Suzy's mother admonished.

However uncertain in the future, the present thoughts of that nice Mr. Gibson, alias Pete, were not ambiguous. Seeing Mog, he stopped his incantations, slithered to a halt, leered, winked, wrenched his hand from the catatonic grasp of First Groupie, flourished it to suggest that it was free for Mog whenever she wished to take up the option, then clearly aiming for a full alpha in his role as master of ceremonies, resumed his circular trudge paced to a valiant rendering of:

"The farmer's in his dell.

The farmer's in his dell.

Ee, i, enyoh, the farmer's in his dell."

"I'm not," Suzy declared, eyes flaring, and keeping her hands behind her back.

Mog shrugged. "All right. You don't have to."

Suzy frowned. Victory that came from indifference was unsatisfactory. When she went into battle, she preferred to see blood.

"I'll not be picked!" she shrilled. "I'm allus the dog and they pat. I don't like them patting. 'The child takes a dog. They all pat the dog. Ee, i, enyoh, they all pat the dog.'"

The quotation was delivered with satirical loathing. Mog looked at her, impressed.

"Okay. We can tell them to choose you as the wife."

The child shook her head as haughtily she surveyed the uncritical tripping and trilling. "The farmer takes a wife." First Groupie, with bashful compliance, had relinquished Pete's hand and was being dragged to the center. There her spouse arranged her in a spot to his liking. His practice in maneuvering vehicles in the sand tray appeared to be paying off.

Suzy's contempt was absolute. "I'll not be the wife! I want to be the farmer!"

Mog flinched and wiped away spittle that Suzy's vehemence had shot into her face. "There's no reason why you shouldn't be. When they have finished this one, they can do it again and you can be him."

That drew a grimace, the Suzy Smile Substitute. "With trousers?" she negotiated.

Recalling Suzy's method of supplying that need, Mog told her that trousers were not necessary. Lots of women were farmers and wore skirts.

"No!" the other shrieked. "Not a woman! I want to be a man farmer."

At last Mog understood Suzy's problem. It was not one she had herself, but that was no reason for writing it off. You had to keep an open mind. Avoid prejudice. "Why?" she asked.

"They *pick.*"

For a youngster, that was a remarkable analysis, succinct

and right on the nail. In two monosyllables she had defined male privilege of first-class citizenship and women's acceptance. Mog viewed the other with respect. However, it was essential not to be discouraged; you had to be constructive, Mog urged her. If she really tried, a woman could break the mold and pick too.

But Suzy remained obstinate. "I want to be the farmer. And I'll pick a wife."

It occurred to Mog that Suzy was suffering from a defective education. She needed some elementary instruction in anatomy. Mog approached the task with pioneering zeal.

Suzy's concentration was admirable and she was especially interested in trying out new words. "Penis?" she repeated several times. However, she appeared unconvinced for her eyes went around the group, searching for confirmation. Acknowledging the importance of visual aids to reinforce learning but suspecting that even Pete might refuse to cooperate, Mog suggested an examination of less sensitive material. The other scuttled off. There was a distant bellow from the thin boy. Suzy returned triumphant and dropped Action Man in Mog's lap.

He was an awe-inspiring representation of the unregenerate male. Though his eyes were not exactly a fathomless brown and it would have been stretching a point to say that his lips had a sardonic curl promising a sensuous fullness, his plastic features were appropriately squared off and the surface was bronzed and polished, hinting an occupation without unsavory sweat. Over the painted hair styled by an army barber, the forage cap fitted snugly and, under the combat jersey, the torso narrowed to the waist so conforming to the model shape. Little contrivance was needed to contort his limbs into pugilistic attitudes and he was particularly adapted to wedging a rifle under his arm.

"You'll see in a minute, under all this clobber," Mog assured her, peeling off the belt.

"I'll grow it," Suzy resolved.

Mog sighed. You would not have thought unarguable fact could be so difficult. Fiction never threw up such barriers. There, you simply wrote in the required response. All the same, you did not give up. Suzy's attitude demanded correction. This desire to be male was subversive and would have to be squashed. Tactfully, of course.

"You don't have to grow a penis, because girls have got something better," Mog argued. It was essential that the child did not feel disadvantaged.

"What?"

Mog removed Action Man's jersey and absently stroked the molded chest. "They have a womb inside them to keep the baby before it comes out." She was relieved that Josephine was not present.

Suzy displayed no enthusiasm. She did not identify herself with temporary storage. But watching Mog as she opened the press studs at what was intended to be Action Man's fly, she pretended an interest.

"Has Sindy got one?" she asked.

"Good question. I doubt it." Mog grinned, imagining the fall in sales if chaste, pubescent Sindy were ever permitted to give birth.

"I'll have a penis, like him," Suzy decided.

She stared entranced as Mog drew the trousers over the slim hips. Then her body went limp and she let out a dismal howl that would have put the keening child to shame. Jointed, bronzed, molded, designed for physical prowess, Action Man was a vessel, as it were, without a rudder. He was Sindy's butch sister. His distinguishing member had been left off.

"After that it was a brawl," Mog concluded later to Rainbow Hair. "Suzy was on the floor, kicking and yelling, all systems go and I couldn't switch her off. The noise did not exactly escape attention; everyone gathered around with Suzy's mum at the front red in the face and going spare. It was not an atmosphere conducive to sober explanation. In any case, I felt a bit of a wally standing there holding Action Man stripped to the buff."

"I can appreciate that must have been difficult to follow up."

"She went on for ages, until Pete offered to let her have a go with his electric drill. You'll not believe how quickly everyone scattered. The drill was a good idea; it was less deafening than Suzy, though the floor is now somewhat pitted. The thin boy took Action Man and dressed him up again. I nearly asked for his opinion on the morning's discovery, but he's a nervous, shy child and I didn't want to give him nightmares about castration."

"That would never do," Rainbow Hair agreed.

It struck Mog that he was not entirely with her. Even the Trev and Mike episode had teased out hardly a grin and before that, when she had described the evening with Denis, he had not been bursting with comment. Or, put it another way, he had been practically mute.

"You feeling low?" she asked.

He shrugged. "I'm thinking. Amounts to the same thing."

Trust him to behave like this, Mog said to herself. If he has not got the microphone and rattling away twenty to the dozen, he cuts out. But, to be honest, this had never happened before, although nowadays he did not go on at such length. She did occasionally interpose a word herself. Quite a few, in fact. As today. After which, he had suddenly gone dumb. Worse than Keith. Because with Keith it was understandable; he had nothing to say. Whereas Rainbow Hair was never short of an opinion, a remark, a joke, or at least a murmur to indicate that the antennae were quivering, to show you he had a sympathetic ear. And that's what she had wanted.

"I started today on a low which was not helped by Josephine," she told him. "Then, what with Mike and Suzy, it began to look up."

"Bully for you."

"Funny how, one way or another, the day has been devoted to sex," she tried again. Perhaps that might enliven him.

"Not my day," he answered.

"Metaphorically, of course."

Nobody would claim that was side-splitting but he might at least have managed a nod. She told him. He nodded.

It was humiliating to make all this effort and meet such resistance. Soon she would be as bad as Dona and Crystal. Correction: for "soon" read "never." She had no need to please him, not being desperate to attract. When she had caught him up outside the college and said she was walking home, it was because she wanted to talk to him; he had not been obliged to accompany her. He should have mentioned that he was not inclined to listen. "I'm thinking," he could have said. "It's my slot in the day for thought. Usually thought and speech for me are synonymous, but every day at four-fifteen I give the old jaw muscles a rest." Still, this afternoon he could have made an exception. It cannot be often that he hears a girl explain her latest problem with our Glenda's library books and he is treated to an analysis, BOOKS and FACT, the latter illustrated with a description of one male–female encounter which Nan Glen would have designated field work.

"Well, thanks for the contribution. You've given me a lot to ponder on," she said.

"And you."

They had reached the end of her street. Mog stopped. "I live down here."

"Which one?"

"The house with a tarpaulin roof."

"Is that a permanent feature?"

"It may become one. My father's opening up the attic."

"Looks as if he may have gone too far."

They were both lingering. The words were inconsequential but an excuse to remain.

"He always goes too far; he has no sense of proportion."

He nodded and, for a reason she did not understand, smiled.

The pallet of brash dyes had almost gone now and the colors had drained to the edge, a ring of brittle tufts. Above, the hair sprang unstained from the roots, a cap uniformly brown, nondescript, unspectacular, and modest.

"The dye is growing out. I've always called you Rainbow Hair to myself. Funny that I don't know your name."

"Bysshe." He grimaced. "But it could have been worse: Percy. My mother had a schoolgirl crush on Shelley."

"A name to live up to."

"I try."

Still neither moved. While Mog's stomach churned. There could be no explanation for that but hunger; it was over three hours since she had had a bite.

"Like to come in for a cup of coffee?" she asked.

The pause was infinitesimal, Mog assured herself later, but the sort in which you live a full week.

"No, thanks. Though I take your point that you have canceled your ruling against men—I refer to question six—I think you should try to retain your sense of proportion. Bye."

Why should I? Mog asked herself, trying to ignore the gastric turbulence. It must be hunger. Also, she appeared to be suffering from other disorders; it was hard walking down the street on rubberized legs. At the moment her condition was D minus minus, give or take a bracket. Either she was growing geriatric or recent experiences were affecting her system, because she felt wrecked. There was a real chance that she would never rediscover the old bounce and optimism. Once, when she was young, she had really believed that there was scope for an alpha in every day.

There was not scope for an alpha in any day for Fred. He was standing at a lamppost wagging his tail at a pair of cats ostentatiously manicuring their claws. Relieved at the excuse to terminate their acquaintance, he joined Mog and pattered beside her. But sometimes Fred would be moved by an irrational desire to excel and this occurred when he came to the gate. He drew up, sank on his haunches, measured the distance, and leapt. However, having chosen a vertical trajectory, he landed on the pavestone he had just left. Puzzled, but hoping to suggest that the failure was the result of a last-minute hitch, he settled down to ritualistic scratching under cover of which he gave the matter some thought.

"You'll never do it," Mog told him. "It's at least two feet six."

Whereupon Fred rose, backed across the road, lined himself square with the gate, and set off at a brisk canter. This attempt was more successful but left him looped over the top, seesawing on his belly with legs thrashing. Giving him a charitable push, Mog reflected upon the salesmanship of the breeder who, pointing him out among the litter of Labradors, had advised Cyril in confidence that for someone not looking for anything special, Fred was a bargain.

"I know how you feel," she comforted him as they entered the kitchen. "You're a case of aspiration with talent deficiency. It runs in the family. But you never know. One day we might get it together."

Propped against Ben's transistor was a letter. From the mottled condition of the envelope, his examination had been thorough, but under his prints you could still make out a heart pierced by an arrow.

"Keith must be moving into illustration," Mog commented. Then saw the name: Cupid Books.

"What did I tell you?" she shouted. "It could be we've made it."

Fred, misunderstanding, crouched under the table and howled.

NINE

Mog stood in front of the mirror and considered her reflection. The crimson blusher did not entirely complement the aubergine eye shadow and together they gave her the appearance of the original battered wife, but it was unreasonable to cavil at gifts. Recently the magazines had been concentrating on hair and pimples, so she had been lucky to find this standard makeup, disappeared when the newsagent's lackey was taking a rest.

Soon, Mog told herself, applying Brush'N'Curl mascara, she would be saved this reliance on sales promotion and be able to buy her own kit. That is, if she thought it worth the outlay. Generally a quick smear with an eyeliner was all she bothered with, but there were occasions when a girl could be excused, squirting deodorant at her armpits, for making a modicum of effort. Such as tonight.

Again Mog craned forward and read the letter. Clipped to the edge of the mirror like a telegram in a star's dressing room, it was still legible though it exhibited acute symptoms of stress. They had done a thorough teatime job on it before it could be rescued and though gentle wiping had removed the crumbs deposited by Grace and the grapefruit pips strewn by Cyril, no amount of dabbing could wholly bleach out Ben's jam and there was nothing on the market strong enough to dissolve the mark of Aunt Edith's nose.

"He wears scent," she had declared, inhaling busily. "You want to watch out, our Mag. And never tell me I didn't warn you," she added to Grace.

She could have done without that, Mog grumbled to herself. It was hard enough to persuade her mother to agree without having to explain away scent.

"Why can't he say what he has to in a letter?" Grace had demanded. "I don't like this 'opportunity for a private chat over dinner.' "

"I do."

Grace paled. "Why couldn't it have been a nice cup of tea in a cake shop?"

"He'll be hungry, Mum," Ben had supported, preparing the ground for a music center, roller skates, etc. Not forgetting a new collar for Fred. "Look, he says he'll 'be in the area on business' and expects to be 'tied up all day.' So he'll want a good blow-out. That's why his secretary 'made some inquiries' and came up with the Railway Hotel."

"Best place," his father agreed. "Mind you, I can't speak for the restaurant, but they'll do you a tidy sandwich if you ask. Cut to order, not from a plastic dispenser on the bar. The rooms aren't bad, either. I sold the manager three Happy Dreams Knock Together vanity units last back end and he said they worked a treat."

"He won't be seeing them," Grace said. "He has to drive back to London that night."

About to comment that the intention did not necessarily limit the man's activities, Mog recognized the wisdom of silence. That the meeting would be short was the only fact that reconciled Grace to it and provided her with a tiny consolation during the next weeks.

One of these days, Mog told herself, she would have to take

her mother in hand and find her something else to worry about. Constant attention to her daughter's welfare was growing inconvenient. But retraining had to be deferred until the book was finished; it was amazing how much time it took up. Since receiving the letter she had made it her full-time job. Or almost, because there had been intrusions. Nobody understood what it was like writing a book. According to the general attitude it was not a serious occupation and authors were either drunken dossers scribbling the occasional paragraph on a beer mat, or hermits penning their odes under the stars, or tax exiles who sketched in an outline for secretary and word processor and then lived it up. And if you did not happen to fall into any of those categories, you simply thought out the book in your bath, by some telemetric method got it on paper, and were free for the rest of the day. Free to attend classes, write essays, do your weekly rota duty in the day nursery, and tolerate Josephine's effusions on her latest boyfriend (still unnamed). Apart from Rainbow Hair, a depressing exception, nobody would leave her alone to do her own thing; a complaint Grace often made, which was an early indication of paranoia. It must be catching.

Perhaps these sorts of demands are the penalty for being an author, Mog shouted above the noise of the hair dryer. But now and again one could have a factor that was so satisfactory that it compensated for the rest. "Satisfactory" was an inadequate description. It was psychedelic, Mog crooned; hysterical, the ultimate, definitely grade A. Through sympathizing with someone else's disappointment she had found a way to zap Mr. Dab.

"I shall be able to help you in the nursery next Tuesday," the earnest woman had said to her; the one who needed a refresher course in contraception, got high on education, and did not wish to be a nuisance. Mog totted up her characteristics for future copy and concluded with: plus a permanent confusion between PULL and PUSH.

"Wrong door," she demonstrated. "Thanks, but there are no gaps next week. Haven't you got German on Tuesday?"

"It's finished. One young lady is having a baby and Mr. Chapman has found a job. Mr. Beadle says he can't justify a class of less than six. I shall miss it; I was so enjoying it, but one shouldn't moan. After all, I have had a taste and I suppose I had taken rather a lot on. You could argue it's something of a blessing," trying to laugh while her face suggested that if this were a blessing, she would be happier with a curse. "The house needs a good clean and my husband is always wittering on that he can't find his socks."

It would be simpler if they bought a decent bloodhound and trained it, Mog thought; reduce a lot of marital stress. But sensing the moment was not quite right for the advice, she postponed the husband's difficulties and concentrated on the class.

There are people walking about who hate controversy, Mog had groaned to herself during the next few minutes. No matter what she said, the woman could not be persuaded to complain. In fact, when that was suggested, she nearly threw a fit. "It's a decision for Mr. Beadle," she quavered. "After all, we are only the students."

Mog twirled the hair dryer and stared into the mirror, letting her jaw drop into an idiotic sag. What can you say to a woman who thinks the school is there for the Principal and is nothing to do with the students? Mourning, she had been disturbed by the insidious thought that perhaps the woman would be better employed cleaning her house and playing hunt the sock. But no, she had rebuked herself firmly that morning. Whatever the discouragements, the fight must go on. Closing the German class midterm was inexcusable.

German. Mr. Dab's subject. Which he rarely taught, leaving

his classes to grub through textbooks and abandoning his group, declaring that self-help was sound education and that in any case their number did not merit his presence.

> . . . A shiver passed through her. It was frightening, etc. but she knew at that moment that an idea, like a child, had been born . . .

It had not taken long to persuade Mr. Beadle. Realizing that her proposal demanded subtle diplomacy, Mog did not linger over her opinion of his decision—you have to make concessions at times—but adopted a positive approach. The Principal had expressed an unreserved enthusiasm; indeed, it suddenly turned out that he had always been a strong advocate for liaison between the college and school. Just as he was happy to have former pupils of Mr. Dab's in his college, herself Floggle being a notable example, so he was confident that Mr. Dab would welcome Nathaniel Chubb students into his group. Mog chose not to disabuse him; her purpose would not be assisted by truth.

"But first I think I should clear it with the education officer before approaching Mr. Dab," the Principal added, revealing a craftiness that was necessary but slightly worrying. Had she misjudged him all these weeks? Mog wondered, and remarked the nails

> . . . professionally manicured without a hint of effeminacy . . .

as he spun the dial. "I think I can rely on the officer's approval," he had assured her, wedging the mouthpiece under his chin. "Indeed, if required, his authorization. There are ways and means. I have to thank you, Tog, for pointing out that I had at my disposal such a practical and imaginative solution."

Mog would have liked to remind him that it had not been at

his disposal until she had suggested it, but he was already making manifest this latest example of Vision to the education officer at the other end of the line.

As Great-aunt Edith would say, he needed watching. But the incident had provided a useful small scene for the next chapter of *An Anatomy of Passion* though, as you would expect, her Principal did not need other people's ideas; she had them all herself.

Later the earnest woman, taking gratitude to excess, had bought her a cup of tea and a Mars bar. No thanks, she claimed, were enough. Nor could she describe to Mog how excited she was to be resuming German and how marvelous it was to be taken under Mr. Dab's wing. Mog thought that paunch was more like it, but offered no correction.

"Of course, Mr. Beadle will be keeping in touch and supervising our progress," the woman had added.

So at last Dab was cornered. The knowledge had given the Mars bar an extra tang.

Mog dug the brush into her hair, screwed down to the scalp, and fired a round from the dryer. She had never appreciated that a blow wave was so tricky; or painful, wincing as she dragged at the brush. She should have aimed for something less ambitious than a

> . . . slinky style with a hint of mystery in the heavy tress which cascaded from the pretty hair slide in a burnished wave which concealed a brow . . .

In her case, for "brow" read "eye." The usual wash, rub, and shake might have been adequate, plus jeans and a T-shirt, if you paid strict attention to the letter. Unraveling the hairbrush and driving a comb through the knots, Mog recited: "Dear Margaret, I hope you will forgive the informality but we are not a very *formal* firm." All the same, she had decided to do herself up a bit. Les had "read the first three chapters with great enjoyment" and would very much like to see her. Pressure of work did not generally allow him to meet their authors, but since he planned to be up in her part of the world etc. Naturally he could not make a definite offer on three chapters, so if she had any more he could look at, he would be delighted . . .

He'll be delighted all right, Mog told herself. It won't be every day that a novel like hers drops on his desk. Chapters four and five had been, as you might say, transitional, but after that letter the next four had really taken off. And they had been written inside a fortnight!

"Here you see before you," Mog trilled happily to her reflection, "not only a human word processor but one dedicated to Art."

The first reward being a dinner at the Railway Hotel with an editor from Cupid Books called Les D'Arcy, and you had to agree that was an improvement on the school cafeteria. She wished there had been time to have her ears pierced because a cascade of earring would look well with Josephine's off-the-shoulder blouse. Unfortunately it could not throw into relief the tan of a long hot summer, but you could not have everything. You had to accept that for some of the time Les might want to talk about the book.

"You've got a visitor," Grace interrupted. "For a moment I thought it might be *him,* but it isn't. I've put him in the front; there's no room in the kitchen with your dad gluing up his Insta-Bond Teleview Sofa. My goodness, Maggie, did you have to do all that? I had hoped you'd go in your old school uniform; I don't want that man to get any ideas. Really, by the look of you, I'd say you and Keith make a good pair."

Though naturally objecting to her mother's last comment, Mog had to admit that there was some truth in it, for lolling against a pile of cartons that held the materials for Cyril's latest project was a young man whose appearance had undergone a startling metamorphosis. Gone were the school tie, blazer, and nondescript trousers, and they had been replaced by a wardrobe of junk, the criteria for each garment being its geriatric condition and the imminence of its falling apart. So a good deal of Keith was visible: toes protruded from the threadbare tennis shoes; a thigh surfaced through a hole in the plus fours; a pectoral muscle was framed by a slash in the tie-dyed vest; and the U.S. Army shirt, worn as a jacket, had been amputated at the elbows to reveal a sturdy arm. Mog was seeing more of Keith than she had done in two years' acquaintance, and none of it pimpled. For him it amounted to indecent exposure. All that, plus earring, digital watch, bangles, and braid, had been achieved by a university in less than two months! Imagine what marvels it might work by the end of his course!

"You're looking different, Maggie," he greeted. "What've you done?"

The question suggested that the result of her labors was an unobtrusive enhancement. "Nothing special," she told him.

Keith shook his head then scrutinized her, frowning. "I know," he reported at last, "it's the skirt. Right?"

So much for the subtle enhancement. "Don't let it worry you, Keith."

"You were always encased in denims. The skirt's okay. Doesn't cover the legs."

This was astonishing. Then she reminded herself that he was a medical student.

"You mean it's more healthy?"

"Mmm. Less risk of allergies. For everyone concerned." He held his face expressionless, but there was a movement along the eyelids which in anyone else would have betrayed a joke.

Even so, she had an uncomfortable sense that Keith had some kind of advantage; there was the need to level the score. "I can't say you're looking so different," she told him.

"That's what everyone says; and my mother assures me that there will always be a bed for me at home." This time she knew he was laughing. "One all, Maggie."

"I wasn't aware we were having a fight."

"No, we aren't. I would not want that, not even now."

Not even now. Not even now she had given him up. Mog stared back at him and felt sad.

"Would you like a cup of coffee?"

"Your mother said you are going out."

"Yes; but I've time."

"Don't bother. Going anywhere special?"

"I'm having dinner in ten minutes at the Railway Hotel."

The news was received without astonishment. "A pity. I'm free till eight-thirty. It would have been nice to have a short chat."

From a young man whose ambition had once been to marry her, set up house with her, supervise the purchase of hardware and the nurture of three wailing brats, this was too casual. He already had something on and was fitting her in. And only a few seconds ago he had made her feel miserable, wondering whether she had been fair to him, wondering whether there had been things she had missed such as a sense of humor and bizarre urges he had chosen to repress, wondering whether it was possible for them to begin again. When the truth was, he had quite got over it; now, she was merely a way of filling in time. You could expect this of a man; few had Mr. Rochester's alleged capacity for everlasting devotion. Not that she had it, either; so far. But she had made no claim to it. She had not rhymed out dozens of tacky poems.

"Sorry to disappoint you," she answered. "But before you go, you can have these back."

In making room for the cartons, Cyril had stacked up the furniture and her haversack was clamped under an armchair precariously inverted over the settee. The need for care thwarted swift action comparable to tearing off a ring and throwing it at his feet, but when she finally gained the haversack, Mog did the next best thing and emptied it on the floor. There was no flutter of poems among the shed contents and she had both hands dredging the mess before she remembered.

"What are you looking for?" he asked, on his knees beside her.

Mog did not answer, pretending to rummage. Because now she regretted the impulse; it was cheap, a petulant attempt at revenge in the style of Dona or Crystal. Whatever your opinion of their fulsome sentiment, the poems had been sincere and, to him, more than an arrangement of words. It was lucky she had handed them to Nan Glen. Still kneeling, she tried to fabricate a plausible lie to Keith's question.

But that was not needed. "Where did you get this?" he asked.

"I borrowed it from a guy in school."

"Has he an ulterior motive for lending it?"

It's a day for surprises, Mog told herself, gaping. You would expect a question like that from Denis, but when it came from Keith and was accompanied by a grotesque wink, a girl could be excused for feeling nonplussed. And it was not only that Keith had made the great imaginative leap to associate your actual couples in the flesh with the textbook illustrations, but he was examining these with a thoroughness that even Trev and Mike would have been pushed to emulate. Perhaps it is his medical training, she argued. There could be no other reason since never before had he revealed such an interest.

"I wanted it for research. I'm writing a book."

Again he received her news without flattering exclamation. He was distinctly laid back. "Good. I always thought you ought to. If writing a book is anything like talking, then you'll have no problem. I can't recall your ever being short on words."

She was, however, at that moment. Though she had to admit his candor bore no malice. She would have liked to mention that going on the evening's form his conversational grade had shot up, but was prevented.

"This appears to be a very conscientious presentation of the subject," he was saying, as if introducing the book to a tutorial of eager students. "But I think it should be approached with caution."

"I can't imagine you approaching it with anything else." Candor was not his prerogative.

"I mean accepting what it claims," he explained, unruffled. "On the face of it I would have thought some of these positions are anatomically impossible. And there is no tabulation of them vis-à-vis desirable age. You can assume a certain gymnastic ability in younger age groups, but I would predict a real danger to older people adopting these positions."

Later, recalling, Mog was able to laugh. Then she was irritated by the lecture. "I'm not bothered whether they spring a hernia. I'm looking at it to help me get descriptions exact."

"Then it's no good relying on this book," Keith said briskly. "You'll have to give it a try yourself. Like we do in the labs."

"You give *this* a try in the labs?"

"Not as yet. I meant experiment in general. On the other hand, according to fifth-year students . . ." He was pushing her stuff into the haversack, his eyes going around the room, assessing the space. "You don't suppose we could shift those cartons into the hall, do you?"

"No. Why?"

"Conditions are a bit cramped. Sloppy attention to detail can prejudice the success of an experiment."

"Are you suggesting we have a go now? Cold? It's obscene!"

Keith tutted and wedged the magazine rack in the hearth. "It's the positions you're interested in, isn't it? In any case," looking at his watch, "I haven't time for anything else. I've this date at half past."

"And I've got one practically this minute." Les would be striding up and down the hotel lounge, watching the door as he sipped a cocktail. Gnawing impatiently at the cherry on the stick.

"It shouldn't take long. You need to get it right and I'm game. It's not often you have a chance for a purely scientific experiment along these lines."

"You can say that again."

"All right, then. I think this would be a good one to start with," pointing. "There should be enough room, except we might be rather pinched when it comes to rolling over. Look, see what I mean?"

They were crouched on the floor, the book between them. The position Keith suggested had a baroque interest.

"I can't see where she puts her left leg," Mog puzzled. His enthusiasm was catching. If Les felt lonely he could stand himself another drink.

"Over his hip, so," Keith worked out, yanking her to him. "We'd get on better if you took your clothes off."

"I'm all ready to go out!"

"But it is essential to do it as illustrated! You can't possibly run an experiment if half the factors are incorrect." He leaned forward and untied the string of Josephine's peasant blouse.

"But why only me? I don't see you peeling down to the buff."

"Naturally I'm going to," throwing off the U.S. Army surplus shirt. But seeing the blouse slipping down her arms and noting the appearance of a Marks and Spencer bra, Keith seemed willing to postpone his disrobing in the interest of hers. In fact he went so far as to ease the blouse out of her skirt and try to lift it over her head. Mog thought that his commitment to research was growing excessive. Which had its attractions.

"I'm not sure that we ought," she delayed weakly.

"I am."

It struck Mog that, while Keith's movements were still businesslike, they now lacked a quality of detachment.

"Look, Keith, my mum or dad might come in any minute. How do you think we should look, trying out positions in the nude?"

"Forget these bloody positions," he said, his arms suddenly round her and one hand fumbling with the zip on her skirt.

There could be little doubt that Keith's interest in conducting a purely scientific experiment had taken a more personal turn. Sweat stippled his brow and his breathing had gone distinctly asthmatic. The saintliness so much admired by Josephine had been recanted and he was making a bid for mischief, vice, sin, dissoluteness, libertinage, lasciviousness. Or—not to put too fine a point on it—lust. In other words, he was exhibiting symptoms inconsistent with the objectivity you expect from a medical man. She told him so.

"I'm not a medical man yet," he reminded her, grasping a thigh in a way that could not be confused with a massage of her sartorius. "I've another four and three-quarter years before I have to maintain a professional objectivity to the female form."

Encouraged by his findings to date, he was preparing to demonstrate how he intended to occupy the next four and three-quarter years, but his plans did not allow for Mrs. Dermot. There were footsteps in the hall, then a face round the door, startled, blushing and instantly withdrawn.

"He's just a *friend,*" Mog insisted a few minutes later. "Only he gets excited telling me about his course."

Her mother's glazed eyes were fastened on a pile of ironing, an eternal verity from which she could derive support. "I forget what his course is."

"Medicine."

Mrs. Dermot groped for a stool. "Sometimes, Maggie," she whispered finally, "I wish I could take to gin."

TEN

If Grace is like that now, by the end of the evening she will be
on a drip, Mog chuckled to herself as she rushed down the
street. According to her mother's vibrant imaginings, the restaurant of the Railway Hotel was a moral minefield compared
with the floor of the Dermot front room. Which at moments
had been pretty ace; but, despite that, spoiled by unexpected
reservations. Why couldn't I go for it, absolutely, one hundred
percent? she asked herself. After all those months when she
had made such an effort, you would have thought Keith's sudden conversion would have freaked a girl out. It was a pity she
had not come across the book earlier; but if she had, there
might never have been Denis or Rainbow Hair. Rainbow Hair.
Who was called Bysshe. Who had said about question seven
that he was having trouble with it himself.

But she could not think about that. It would have to wait.
Sometimes there was so much to think about that, as Great-
aunt Edith said, you might wear out your brain. Not that
G. A. Edith had one to risk. For the last two weeks, though,
what had occupied most of her thoughts had been dinner with
Les. And now it was about to happen. The Railway Hotel was
in sight. Mog paused, studied her face in Josephine's mirror,
adjusted her eyeshade of hair, and added another coat of En-

riched Special Performance lipstick. Then, brushing past a car transporter, a mobile blood-doning unit, and a cement mixer parked opposite her goal, Mog crossed the road and climbed up the steps.

Immediately, as

. . . the full realization of what she was about to do came upon her, she felt her brain swim. Her legs turned to jelly under her and she leaned upon the gilt balustrade for support. Behind her was the golden-sanded beach, lipped by the gentle kissing waves of the lagoon in which was reflected the moon, for all the world like an enormous luminous plate set on the midnight blue cloth of the tropical sky. Before her were the subdued glow, the ankle-deep carpets and the secret murmur of couples in the expensive Yachting Club, where waited for her the man who was tied to her heart by indissoluble knots. Could she be sure that his passion equaled hers? Had he gone further than he meant in that simple but eloquent signature on his letter, "Yours, Les?" Tonight would be the test. She had prepared herself so carefully for him. She had put on an unpretentious but elegant drawstring blouse that showed off to perfection her pretty shoulders. She had acquired some new, fashionable makeup. Would that be enough? Tears sprang to Juliet-Bella's eyes as she thought how much better she could have dressed if all her Great-aunt Edith's assets had not sunk with her long ago on that fateful morning in the Irish Sea. She had been Juliet-Bella's only surviving relative. But this will never do, she reproved herself, and her eyes cleared. He waits for me in the vestibule; and would he be the same man who appeared to her every night in her dreams? Tall, handsome, leaning with casual grace against the mantelpiece, the heart-stopping Les D'Arcy, immaculate in his wild silk tie and handmade shoes . . .

This evening, however, Les D'Arcy was more adequately covered, wearing a neat jersey two-piece suit and beige sling-backs.

"You must be Margaret," she said. "Your description of yourself does not do you justice."

They shook hands, Mog feeling in need of a balustrade for support. At last she was able to stutter: "I'm sorry I'm late. I was held up."

"And you don't have to tell me by whom." Les D'Arcy smiled brightly.

Mog accepted her permission. This occasioned a brief pause.

"Shall we go in?" the other asked, the smile eclipsed. But it was out again by the time their table was reached.

"So here we are," she pronounced, stroking the back pleats of her skirt into position and lowering herself gently into the chair. "And what an ideal place this is for a private chat!" A hand, much ringed, gestured around the unoccupied room.

Ideal was not the word Mog would have applied to it since there were no candles on the tables to replace the raw light of the fluorescent tubes, no single bloom floating in a cut-glass dish to compensate for the bottle of tomato ketchup, no seductive perfume to offset the stench of boiled cabbage, no gliding waiters, no backless evening gowns, no musical laughter, no crescent of floor satin-polished for dancing behind which talented instrumentalists softly rendered a magical, dulcet tune. These were worrying indications that the evening, already failed in one expectation, might not come up to scratch. Mog tried to redress the balance by studying the à la carte menu and, as a suitable aperitif, deciding on a bacardi and rum.

"I think the table d'hôte is more to our purpose," Les D'Arcy stated and, reaching for the carafe of water, poured

Mog a glass. "It *is* hard to make up one's mind," she sympathized as Mog stared gloomily at the waitress. "Shall we have the beef casserole? And begin with the soup of the day. What is it?"

Soup of whose day? Mog thought, and wondered what ingredient the Railway Hotel would choose for celebrating hers. They must have a suitable emetic.

Meanwhile Les D'Arcy was prattling cheerily. "Now I want to know all about you. It isn't often we receive a script from someone so young. And such an attractive young lady, too. I'm sure you must have lots of boyfriends?"

"I've given them up," Mog mumbled automatically.

"Ah; I see." Les D'Arcy nodded tolerantly like a Sister on a psychiatric ward listening to a new patient. "There has been some unhappiness?"

Mog thought. "Not particularly," she answered. "More like dissatisfactions."

This was less credible. "It can be a mistake to expect that one's first choice is the right one," the other said briskly.

It occurred to Mog that she had never chosen Keith. She said so.

"How very right you are!" Les D'Arcy intoned sagely. "In matters of the heart one rarely stands back and makes a conscious choice. It is a delicate intuitive process over which we have little control, and we can put all our future at risk by saying it nay."

Mog would have liked to correct the other's misunderstanding by emphasizing that her delicate intuitive process had definitely said nay to Keith. Until that evening. Now it was just possible it had been wrong, but confusing Les D'Arcy would have to wait. This late eating was holding up the three-hourly input of energy.

There appeared little chance that would be provided by the soup. A transparent saline solution weakly tinted by a vegetarian beef cube, it suggested that the chef interpreted the day as cool, wet, and polluted by smog. This was confirmed by its taste. Trying not to retch, Mog considered that it might not be advisable to lever Grace out of her kitchen; in a straight competition with this preparation, she would win a pure alpha.

Les D'Arcy enjoyed no such comparison. "What a delicious consommé!" she enthused, slurping it up.

"Well, you mustn't be disheartened," she advised, referring to those distressing occasions when the intuitive process was taking a rest. "It may be no more than a little tiff. Even the most beautiful relationship is not always exempt from those, although naturally in our books we prefer not to contemplate that possibility. But if this young man really is not Mr. Right, you must not let the disappointment sour your view. We all know what that can lead to. These women with new-fangled ideas, actually *choosing* to set up home by themselves! Most of them living off social security. It's not natural." Les D'Arcy shivered. Mog wondered whether she doubled up editing with running a marriage bureau. "So you can see why I don't like to hear a pretty young lady like you say she has given up men," she concluded, her face stern.

Mog wished she had not mentioned this. For one thing, it clearly won no applause from a representative of Cupid Books and might prejudice her novel's chances, and for another she was no longer sure of her ground. If you defined abstention from men as a diary bereft of engagements, then her claim was true; but if you extended the definition to shunning their company, being impervious to sensations they could provoke, finding no interest in their personalities, and not musing over one in particular, then her assertion was false. This was disturbing. Also, if you were inclined to take honesty to excess, it had to be admitted that the one in particular had never been Denis and was no longer Keith.

. . . At which Juliet-Bella's strong nerves almost snapped . . .

"Forgive me for being so outspoken," Les D'Arcy was saying. "It's a habit. We are a very *outspoken* firm. Cheer up, my dear."

She leaned across the table, reared her head for an oblique scan through bifocals, sighted Mog's hand foraging for another bread cob and, with a clash of rings and tinkle of lucky-charm bracelet, brought it down on the plate. "You are still so very young," squeezing. "Every day, almost every hour, is a new start. And who knows? The young man for you may be only just around the corner."

Before the other grew too lyrical, Mog thought she should mention what lay just round the corner from the Railway Hotel, but instruction on the town's sanitary arrangements was prevented by the appearance of the casserole of beef. It also cut short further squeezing. You can contract gangrene by arrested circulation, Mog rebuked silently, massaging her fingers under the folds of the cloth.

. . . While Bella found herself quite unable to do justice to the exotic dish he had chosen for her, marinaded in the finest Burgundy from the club's deservedly famous cellars and served with tender shoots of out-of-season asparagus, for her hand was like a live thing, aware, dancing to the new, primitive rhythms commenced by his glancing touch . . .

"I suspected something of the sort when I read your novel," Les D'Arcy continued, admiring the wizened features of a rogue brussels sprout. "This girl has *suffered,* I said to myself at the end of the third chapter; the writing springs straight from the heart. I can always spot it. You may not believe me, my dear, but I am quite an old lag at the game." She stopped chewing and tilted her head girlishly. "And it shows," referring to Mog's primary organ, "for without it there can be no true emotion, and that is generally accompanied by suffering, which is a prerequisite of Art. That is, if we take as our mentor the prestigious poet T. S. Eliot."

Sensing that her chosen mentor might bring an unwelcome asperity to the conversation, Les D'Arcy quickly dumped him and carried on. "In fact, it reminded me very much of myself, when I was little older than you. How I suffered, believing that Mr. D'Arcy had no tender regard for me! But it all came right in the end, and we had three marvelous years." Mrs. D'Arcy impaled a rectangle of beef on the prongs of her fork and regarded it meditatively. "Then he was mortally injured in a road accident. I have never wished to remarry. There is not a man on this earth who could replace him."

Shocked, Mog attempted a bar or two of sympathetic noises but, champing on the beef, the other did not hear them. It seemed that an early demise was an occupational hazard for minor characters associated with Cupid Books.

"However, that is a personal digression and I am sure that we should both enjoy a little tête-à-tête, but we are here to talk business, are we not? Nothing sordid, of course, because we are concerned with *love*, but from time to time we have to put our heads together and try to be practical." Mrs. D'Arcy paused, allowed the smile to peep out again, then sucked it back. "You may have noticed, Margaret, that I spoke of the first three chapters. The next six I have read this morning. I must say frankly to you that they leave me astonished."

Mog halted her attempts to tenderize a piece of gristle and let her jaws relax; also the rest of her body. Such a compliment was gratifying. Any more like that, and this meeting would be lifted straight out of grade delta and beyond the finite limit of a score.

"Well, I was trying to be a bit different," she admitted modestly. "I mean, after three chapters I was sick of the heroine; she was like all the rest, chained to a typewriter and wet."

"They don't all do office jobs," Mrs. D'Arcy defended, coughing slightly.

"No; but they have the equivalent; they are never the boss, so I thought it was about time to inject some originality, put her in charge and make the man do the hanging about and worrying how he looks and never knowing from one moment to the next whether she is going to make a pass at him or slap him in the face. Here, you can have my napkin; it's maybe a lump of gravy stuck in your throat," as Mrs. D'Arcy's coughs increased. Anybody would think she was choking.

"It was not easy to graft that on to the first three chapters," Mog confided, "and I did consider scrapping them and starting again but I'm pleased now that I didn't since you like them," for a moment recalling the suffering that came from the heart. "I left them in because I thought it better to show how such a spineless twit could change and I must admit I think I've achieved that."

Mrs. D'Arcy's agreement came on rasping breaths.

"I suppose what I am doing is giving the old formula writing a new look, as Nan Glen put it; she's the course tutor of a creative writing class I attend. I already had the idea, of course, but what she said encouraged me to develop it further. There are a couple of things that have given me trouble, still are doing, but you needn't worry; they'll be resolved," Mog rushed on. It was incredibly pleasurable talking about your work to someone in the trade. "One is the sex. It gets me the way it's done in such a limited fashion. Nan Glen agrees, but she's a proper writer, of course. She's all for precise writing, else you'll never convince, so I'm trying for more realism, which involves research not only in books but, as Nan Glen would say, out in the field. It's coming on, and I expect I'll have it together by the time I reach the relevant chapter." Mog thought it wise to give that assurance. "What you can rely on absolutely is that, for Cupid Books, it will be very advanced. All this being stretched out on silk sheets and downy pillows while skin throbs under his touch and everything is forgotten in an explosion of indescribable ecstasy is simply no go."

Still troubled by a blocked gullet, Mrs. D'Arcy was unable to articulate, but her cheek muscles were seen to pulse feebly. Lip-reading, Mog made out: Late husband a most considerate man.

Not pausing for further intimate revelations, Mog continued. "The sex is easy, really; it's just a matter of getting detail correct. For example, Denis said he wasn't thinking of taking all night and certainly that inclination was endorsed on the second occasion, whereas Keith considered half an hour was not long enough, though there was strong evidence that he was prepared to concede principles in favor of a shorter session. I haven't had the opportunity to try out Rainbow Hair, or Bysshe."

Mrs. D'Arcy was looking distinctly off and the hand clutching her water glass had developed a tremor.

Mog fitted in a swift commiseration on the lines that a bad cough can affect the whole system, then began the final sprint.

"But all that is child's play compared with the second item that has been giving me trouble. It's the whole question of what makes you go for someone and how you behave when you do. I even thought of cutting it out, but I couldn't do that since the book is supposed to be a Romance. *Jane Eyre* came up in the writing class and I used it for working out a set of questions. I'm sorry I haven't brought them; but I can remember what most of them are."

Mrs. D'Arcy flapped a hand, hinting a request.

"All right, we can discuss them in depth later, but by the time I had reached chapter five I was trying to investigate how fancying a man affected the heroine and whether a state of drugged infatuation, with all principles and criticisms blind-folded, is essential for being in love."

The last word produced a remarkable change in her audience. Like a mother conditioned to spring to attention at the demand of her child, Mrs. D'Arcy sat up, relinquished her grip on her glass and again sought Mog's hand. Since it was then latched around a fork on which was balanced a small pyramid of fossilized peas, the table cloth of the Railway Hotel came in for some punishment, but Mrs. D'Arcy did not notice. "Ah, my dear, you have so put your finger on it," she whispered, her lids damp. "People can analyze to their heart's content, but we do not have to be told what love is, do we? We know."

From this, Mog got the impression that Mrs. D'Arcy had not followed her argument and what faint interest she may have had in it had been renounced for a thorough exploration of Mog's hand. This involved considerable massage and kneading which was not entirely clinical.

Mog tried to redirect the other's attention. "What I can't go a bomb on is the way these women are so excessive," she explained. "They lose all their independence. They're happy for him to take over and dominate, provided that he can persuade them that he is eternally theirs."

Spoken close, for by this time Mrs. D'Arcy's head was bobbing above the tomato ketchup, the words found their target. For a moment Mrs. D'Arcy was still, then her hand scrambled back and was dropped in her lap.

"Are you telling me that you are a *feminist?*" she demanded.

Mog considered the question irrelevant but gave it thought. "I'd call myself a democrat. I mean, there are moments when I admit that my dad . . ."

"Do you suppose I can go into my chief and suggest we put one of those on our list, whatever name you give yourself?"

Mrs. D'Arcy interrupted, her voice shrill. "I had imagined that, over a nice quiet dinner, we could cut out all that rubbish in the last six chapters—tactful editing is my forte—and get back to chapter three, but I see I was mistaken. I was ready to help you with certain aspects that you needed to bring in, for example, jealousy, which you completely omit. That's a basic ingredient and a sure sign to our readers that a man cares. And let me tell you, they don't want it all spelled out like that woman who runs your writing class." Here Mrs. D'Arcy gave a loud snort. "They are looking for a few hours' escape from all that. And that's what Cupid Books give them. And they don't wish to read about babies in a day nursery, either. That comes after marriage, and they can have it any day. *Love* is what they want to read about, not changing nappies, and while I have my way, that is what they will continue to get."

There was a short silence during which Mog contemplated murder and suicide and dismissed both, mainly because she had no gun handy and the knives of the Railway Hotel were uncommonly blunt.

"You mustn't mind my being so frank," Mrs. D'Arcy concluded.

"That's all right." The lie of the century, that was.

"I knew you would take it in the right spirit." Mrs. D'Arcy smiled and Mog was shocked that she had not recognized before the laser eye, the bludgeoning thrust of the chin.

"It hurts me as much as it does you," the woman assured her. "But sometimes it is necessary to take a book to pieces."

"Do you mind if I go now?"

"Aren't you finishing the entrée? But of course, it is getting late and you have lessons tomorrow. I'm pleased to have met you."

Mog pretended not to notice the offered hand.

At the door she looked back. Mrs. D'Arcy had returned to her congealing dinner and was performing an autopsy upon a recalcitrant chip.

ELEVEN

Mog sat in the school library and reread the letter she had just written.

> *Dear Keith,*
>
> *When you came round a fortnight ago there was something I should have told you, that I had given three of your poems to Nan Glen, who runs a writing class I attend. Since they are personal I know I should not have done that, but I was in rather a difficult position at the time—I won't bore you with details—and I had to pretend I had written them myself. It was a necessary expedient, the sort you have to use occasionally to get out of a tangle. By which I mean that I have to, not you. I don't know whether you have noticed. Anyway, last night Nan Glen said they are "promising" and offered to send them to a magazine. Of course, I owned up.*

"I thought as much," Nan Glen had said. "They do not sound as if they were written by a woman."

Two weeks earlier Mog would have judged Keith incapable of coloring anything with his masculine gender but after the Scientific Experiment and Josephine's news that morning, many assumptions were proving unreliable. Still, she had been puzzled.

"There is nothing mysterious in that," the other explained, seeing her face. "I have only picked up the obvious indications. For example, a woman does not usually speak of the fire in her loins."

"Did he say that?" She had missed it, eight lines scribbled on the back of the poem admitting to voluptuous thoughts.

> *I decided that you would not mind if I let Nan Glen type them and send them off, and I will let you know what happens either way. I asked her to cut out the "To Maggie."*

I wish I had not done that, she moaned to herself; after all, they were written to *me*. And if I think much more about them I shall start crying, bubbling away like Great-aunt Edith watching *Love Story* or Josephine reading *Jane Eyre*. Which is strong evidence that I have reached a new low.

"It must have been the blouse," Josephine had reported. "You know, the one I lent you for dinner with that Les D'Arcy, and I can tell you it went down better with Keith than it did with her. He said he'd seen it somewhere before, but I told him it was only a Littlewoods so there are thousands about."

"I didn't know you were going out with him."

"We weren't exactly, at first, and I didn't like to say. It was a bit awkward since he had been your boyfriend. Especially after what you had said. And I don't find him like that at all."

"How do you find him?"

"I was hoping you'd ask."

On such occasions Josephine's description was lavish, which made Mog regret her request. The encomium covered all features ending with: "And if that isn't enough, there's his body!"

"I'm surprised you've got to that."

Josephine giggled. "Funny how you remember things. It suddenly came back to me, you talking about the men in those books having an untanned strip, as yet unrevealed. I told Keith. We had a good laugh."

"Feel free." Any more of this and she would need a new set of teeth. Perhaps G. Aunt Edith could oblige.

"No, honestly; it's funny."

"Was Keith's?"

"How do you mean? Oh . . . I didn't see."

At any other time Mog would have found this comic. The previous morning her reaction was, oddly, relief. This she explained by: "I was growing anxious. For someone who says she would not trust any of them an inch, there's been a vast change." Brought on by *Keith?*

"Ah, but Keith is different." Josephine's voice was decidedly tacky. "Did you know he's been coming down alternate weekends? His dad is teaching him to drive, then we can borrow his car. I've never had a boyfriend with wheels."

"I'd rather have them with legs." Rotten, but all she could manage.

"His dad says he'll make a good driver, but you would expect that; he's got so many talents. And he says, why do a job by halves? Mind you, at the time he was talking about a book on sex."

"That will be part of his required reading." It was a necessary try.

Josephine found this hilarious. Her idea of what was funny had clearly deteriorated under the influence of Keith. "Well, yuss, but not for lectures. More for extramural activities."

"In the nature of pure scientific experiment." You had to keep fighting.

There was a pause during which Josephine added another hundred decibels to the laughter track and Mog chewed at her cuticles with the stumps of teeth. Eventually Josephine gasped out that Mog was a laugh; nearly as good as Keith. He had remarked that he had had a go at experiment once, but the result had been disappointing. Apparently he was confident that with more serious application they could get it right.

Having no wish to hear about Keith seriously applying himself, Mog had pleaded an English class; they were about to discuss the sexual content of *King Lear*. Perhaps Josephine would care to join them. Not surprisingly, the invitation had been declined.

> *It was nice seeing you again and having your news. Jose-phine tells me you are learning to drive. The best of luck with that, anyway.*
>
> Caio, Maggie

That "anyway" was revealing, but she could not bear to copy out the letter again. She had had trouble with the last paragraph. Reference to their "little romp surrounded by Dad's cartons of knock-together furniture" introduced a pleasing air of sophistication but invested the occasion with more importance than Mog wished. Also, she had deleted the comment that she understood it was Josephine who was now in his voluptuous thoughts and no doubt providing fuel for the fire in his loins. It was satisfactorily bitchy but unjustified. Neither of them was responsible for what she felt, because it was through her that Keith had seen the book and was planning to put it into operation with Josephine. You could not blame them when she found that ironic. If Josephine had guessed, she would not have talked as she had. They had been friends since nursery school. Soon she really would cry.

As she folded the letter she was aware of someone taking the chair opposite her.

"Don't worry; I'm not reading it, but I did catch the name. Is he new?"

She shook her head. "Before your time."

Licking a finger, Petal Bysshe drew an exclamation mark on the surface of the table. "An ambiguous response, he thought to himself. Had he ever enjoyed a time? He would have asked her to clarify but was feeling hung over. It struck him that her eyes, too, lacked their customary luster. Could there, he asked himself, be anything wrong?"

"You've taken your time to reach that question."

"Rhetorical, he assured her." His eyes were on the letter.

"This is only part of it. It's been a bad month." Then, "It's ages since I saw you."

"He protested that he'd been around."

"I don't mean for a quick hello in the corridor. I mean to talk."

"He sighed silently to himself and a nerve flicked under one of his wide-set peat-bog brown eyes. Because did this woman ask only talk of him? Had he nothing else to offer her? He knew—no one better—that in all essentials he was a man as other men, yet she preferred . . ."

"Are you sloshed?" Mog demanded.

"Don't you like it? Thought it might ring a bell."

"It does, and I don't want to know. That's what I'd like to tell you about."

"You're saying that you want *you* to talk? Look, I've no objection in principle but there are drawbacks . . ."

"Will you wrap up! I want to tell you about Les D'Arcy."

"Not another!"

"What?"

"That's the drawback. I don't mind listening, Mog, but I'd be happier if you'd cut out the erotic scenes. It's just a preference. I have this hang up about obligatory voyeurism."

She could not imagine what he referred to. "Erotic scenes?" Perhaps Josephine had recounted the story. "You mean when Les D'Arcy stretched over the table and grabbed my hand, like this, and squeezed and I couldn't pull my fingers away from hers?"

"Hers?" Interest was kindled. There was even a touch of color in the face. Trust a man to brighten up at mention of a woman. "Spare me nothing," Bysshe permitted magnanimously. "Tell me all."

Mog did.

"I'm sorry, but I can't help finding it funny," he told her.

"Is that all you can say?" She would have liked to give point to her annoyance by withdrawing her hand but she did not want the fuss. When she had reached across and taken his, she had only intended to demonstrate Les D'Arcy's behavior, but he had continued to hold on.

"Is that a serious question? That I might have only the one sentence of comment?" He was grinning, mocking them both. "You could write a book about it. Sorry. A sore point. What I'm saying is, it throws up so much we could go on for hours."

"Yes." She could not suppress the hope.

He was examining her hand, smoothing around a bitten cuticle with his thumb. Please, Mog groaned, don't let it be another case of: "Dear Ruthy, My boyfriend is only interested in my health forever taking my temperature and seeing me as a patient not a normal woman and saying I suffer from a hyperactive libido and he will get me a prescription."

Then he slid his hands away and looked around. "But we haven't even minutes," he said briskly. "Haven't you remarked that Hard Man Sugden is making delicate hints that we vacate the library? Note that he has stacked the chairs on this table and is braced to remove these from under us if we don't clear out."

So, forlorn, Mog walked with him down the corridor.

At the main entrance he said, "Apart from everything else, what about the writing?"

"That's over. She wouldn't take it as it is."

"I gathered that, but shall you try again?"

"No."

"Oh, come on, Mog, don't be put off so easily. However it turned out, it was useful experience."

"I can't do it."

"I don't mean for Cupid Books, you soft thing. I never expected you could write one for them. Against the grain for a girl like you." Then he was leaning into her, smiling. Her arm was grasped lightly. "Particularly when she has given up men!"

"I wish you'd stop saying that. It wasn't a joke. And you shouldn't have read what I wrote. It was private. If you hadn't done, you would never have known."

"I stand rebuked. Justly." The hand had already dropped from her arm. "And as you say, I would never have known. See you."

A few steps along the pavement he stopped. "Sorry about the Les D'Arcy disappointment," he said, and paused as if about to say more. Then again: "See you," and walked away.

It is about time he could think of another farewell, Mog raged to herself; I'm sick of this casual "See you." Also, any more teasing about giving up men and I'll go berserk. He seems to think that it is impossible, that men are a commodity you can't be without. It is so conceited, it's enough to make a girl renew the no-man pledge. I would say I don't know why I go for him except, to be honest with myself, I know why I do.

But I don't know why I bother to dissect conversations with him; that is a habit I've developed to excess. For example, today there was all that about cutting the erotic scenes and obligatory voyeurism as if I went in for intimate confessions; and the way he said, "I would never have known," as if I had so many men he would not have suspected I had given them up! When all I've done is told him about Denis, and that was weeks ago. In fact, the last time we had a good talk. Or I did.

Shocked, Mog halted. "No! It can't be!" she said aloud, startling a paper boy and a vagabond cat. But it was.

There are times when you can overdo the historical analysis, Mog told herself wearily five minutes later as she entered her street. No matter how many repeats she did of the story, finding each time a fresh detail to convince herself that it had been a thoroughly objective report on a MALE–FEMALE ENCOUNTER, she had to admit she had been unbelievably crass. She had raced on, preoccupied with Mrs. Kitson's Crystal, her ambivalence during the scramble with Denis, and the issues these raised for her book. Taking his sympathetic ear for granted, she had not thought about Bysshe. Apart from other considerations, most of which she did not feel like examining, it was not exactly tactful to describe what had happened with Denis to a fellow who had once said he was having trouble himself with item seven on her list; and on another occasion, "I have to delay answer until I have the complete scenario to go on but I'm working on it." And it was no good saying that the question was, "What the hell is love?" and telling him that with Denis it was only lust. Now he assumed that Denis mattered. It was ironic, like Keith's introducing Josephine to the borrowed book on sex.

She had never felt so miserable and she did not know what she could do. Generally she could haul herself out of the morass by attempting something constructive, but imagination was defunct. It was a case of terminal inertia. Perhaps she needed a brain transplant.

"It throws up so much, we could go on for hours," he had said, then afterward he had remembered. There was nothing in her experience that could suggest a remedy. And Dona and Crystal offered no help. In fact, they often went out of their way to provoke such a situation, even setting it up, persuading some compliant stool pigeon to play a game with them so that their cut-rate Mr. Rochester should be jealous, grab, and pant out eternal love. Mog paused, her legs unsteady. Had she made Bysshe jealous? Surely not! He did not seem the type. Jealousy she could not condone, for which reason it had not figured in *An Anatomy of Passion*. An omission Les D'Arcy had wanted her to correct. All the same, he might be jealous, Mog told herself grimly; and if so, she had managed with him what she had been unable to do in the book. That was a good example of fact triumphing over fiction. Also, another irony. She was into irony today. It was bruising. For pulverizing the emotions, knocking out the mind, and bringing on heart failure, there is nothing like a workout with yourself as punching bag.

What I need, she told Fred as she unscrewed his head from the cat door, is a three-course snack and a cozy evening at home, my aching brow resting upon the family bosom, the day's cares salved by mindless domestic chat or, better still, by the peace arising from a Grace–Cyril freeze in communication. But the family was uncooperative.

They were gathered in the kitchen waiting and Ben pounced before she had closed the door.

"Mag, there's been vans and cables and lights and cameras and piles and piles of equipment outside the Tech . . ."

"What's happened?" Grace interrupted. "Next door is saying there must have been an incident."

". . . and cameramen and a sort of restaurant on wheels . . ."

"That's because their union checked on the cafeteria," Mog said.

"You mean it's got rats and cockroaches and things?"

"No; only Noreen."

"The one that serves?" Grace came in. "I would not have thought, from what you've said, that she'd look right on television, but you never know, do you? You never know who they might discover next." Agitated by the possibility, she removed her apron.

Mog sighed. "All they are doing is making a short film about the college and it will go out just before Christmas—next week."

"I'll ask Thelma to come round and give you a wash and set," Grace promised. "You'll want to look nice."

"That's not necessary, Mother."

"She's right," Cyril supported. "She'd look silly, especially got up. The TV people will want her looking her usual self, natural."

"They are making a film of the college, not me," she reminded them.

"And you'll have been helping, I expect," her father stated happily, with "if I know my girl" understood.

"I did make a number of suggestions to Mr. Beadle."

"That's my girl," Cyril approved.

However, her advice had not been welcomed. To her surprise, Mr. Beadle was prepared to leave decisions about shots to the director of the program and he had refused her offer to describe changes she had initiated in the school. The scriptwriter had been thoroughly briefed and their school would be presented as an institution in the vanguard of progress, a revolutionary force in the life of every member of its catchment and—who knows?—beyond.

The tone had been confident, but Mog noticed that he had looked exceptionally furtive. Perhaps bribery or coercion was an occupational requirement for the Principal of Nathaniel Chubb, she had thought, remembering that on previous occasions he had mentioned ways and means.

"All that helping has taken it out of her, you can see that," Grace diagnosed. "She's looking tired."

"She's hungry," Mog pointed out.

"That's only to be expected, but I'm afraid it will be a

scratch meal, after hearing this. Fancy! Our Maggie on the TV!"

"Don't rely on it." She had resolved that, having declined her assistance, Mr. Beadle could take full responsibility for making a mess of the program. So she had spent her time avoiding the cameras.

"But of course you will be! They can't be doing without a young girl like you. You'll look nice, sitting behind a desk." Grace cracked an egg into a saucer and sniffed ecstatically. "I can't wait to see it."

Let her convince herself that you are appearing on television and Grace goes delirious, Mog reflected; tell her that you are going to write a book, and she does not want to know. After no more than this slight contact with the box her mother had caught the blight; soon she would come out in spots. And it was infectious.

"Do you think I could be in it, too, Mag?" Ben asked her. "I could pretend to be going to an evening class. Tyron's dad takes their Whiskers to Social Adjustment for the Radioactive Dog. I could take our Fred. He'd like that."

"Hyperactive," she corrected; and then for the first time that day Mog was able to laugh.

TWELVE

It was a rain battered evening in mid-December. Above turbulent gutters, papier-mâché litter and a single aquatic dog, the hands of the town hall clock groped toward the hour. A cog turned feebly in its bed of rust; a spring twitched under its shroud of grime. After a century of neglect the mechanism fought to make a last brave strike, grated, was rattled by spasms, and came to rest. But its decease went unnoticed.

For in front of every television set in the town people were gathering. Fathers laid aside the racing pages and selected the channel; grandfathers backed into armchairs and unbuttoned their collars; mothers pulled off aprons and fetched in the cat; children adjourned play and jostled for space. In the old people's home nurses maneuvered wheelchairs and adjusted blankets; in the public houses men left the dart board and squeezed around the bar set; in the doorway of an electrical shop Albert stacked his plastic bags and peered through the glass. Myrtle took out pad and pencil ready for swift transcript; Mrs. Lewis tucked up her children and ran down the stairs; Hard Man Sugden took a drag at his hip flask and called to Noreen; clutching a box of chocolate liqueurs, Mr. Dab winched himself into a chair. Trevor dragged his eyes from position eighteen; Denis hastened to finish a precourting shave; Josephine added a comma to "Dear Keith" and looked up. All over the town, along streets and terraces, in flats and clubs, in factory cafeterias and the Railway Hotel, the television sets had been switched on. Mr. Beadle's dream of a community college that entered the home of every member of its catchment was now a recognized fact.

There were, however, a few dissenters.

"Haven't you had enough of that place without ogling at it on TV?" Walt demanded, emptying a Wellington boot over Pete's step. "I was fancying a game of billiards at the Fighting Cock. You haven't been the same man since that young lass got you on minding the babbies. All right—so she's a nice bit of crumpet, and brains with it, but that don't mean you have to act soft."

"I don't know why you had to fetch a body out a night like this," Great-aunt Edith grumbled. "I've no objection to sitting in front of that thing now and again but if you suppose I'm perching up like a parrot on that box, then you've got another think coming. And I'm not having that oddity, either. You don't have to tell me our Cyril put it together; I can see that. If you don't mind, I'll have the chair out of the kitchen; it's hard, but I'll manage. I'm not one to make a fuss. Have you put that Fred in the shed? I don't know why I let myself be persuaded. It's only a jumped-up workhouse. I don't know how our Maggie got herself messed up with it. Where is she? I hope she's not gallivanting with that Les again."

"I've told you, Auntie, Les D'Arcy is a woman," Grace said wearily, and bending over the set, turned up the volume.

"Is he now? And our Maggie mixed up with him! What's the world coming to?" watching the other's face.

It paled. Aunt Edith tittered.

"She's watching at a friend's house. He telephoned her about half an hour ago."

"Well, I'll give it to our Maggie, she don't let grass grow under her feet."

"She's known him some time," Grace told her, desperate. "I took the call and I must say he sounded a nice polite young man."

Aunt Edith cackled boisterously. Observing her niece quake, she dipped into the cache of biscuits in her lap and turned her attention to the screen. As the camera glided down a street, found Nathaniel Chubb, fixed on its cramped portals and moved in close, Aunt Edith released a derisive snort, announced loudly, "It's them is nice and polite has got thoughts," and split open a custard cream with her one yellowing tusk.

The thoughts of the nice polite young man were at that moment unprintable, being directed at the intestines of a malfunctioning set.

"We don't have to watch it," Mog told him.

"But isn't that why you are here?"

"If you say, Bysshe."

"I'm saying nothing that might prejudice your conduct, except to remark that you might be more comfortable without the sou'wester, but these things are a matter of personal taste. And do help yourself to the chair. As you see, the landlord has a penitential approach to the furnishing of bed-sits. Either one of each item or nothing. This technological marvel is, of course, my own, and a very restful specimen of the genus, identified by the pattern of crisp candy-stripes."

"I should think the aerial's loose."

"You're right. Mog, before I connect us to the satellite, there's something I want to say."

"I know: if anything survives the explosion we can have it for transplant."

"That, too." He paused. "I'm pleased you wrote that letter.

Thanks." Again he paused, then quickly, "Okay? Are you sitting comfortably. One, two, three . . ."

1. **Street outside Nathaniel Chubb School.** Day. Camera pans along pavement, discovers litter. It rests on a polyethylene cup and small cairn of sodden chips heaped on a crumpled poster with illustration of empty wastepaper basket and caption: "Nathaniel Chubb School—your place. Show how you care." Camera pulls back, to show students walking down school steps, picks out two and follows them across the road, the patch of waste ground and toward the Drayman's Arms. The students wear denims and combat jackets, and have spiked hair. Sex is uncertain but halfway along the path one puts an arm behind the other and massages the neck. **Cut.**

2. **Corridor of School.** Camera swings from wall to wall as though drunk. It moves up corridor and rests on door of men's lavatory. **Fade into:**

3. **Street outside School.** Day. In camera, Presenter with mike.

PRESENTER: *Welcome once again to* Taking the Lid Off, *the program that gives you facts without tears. Today we are visiting Nathaniel Chubb, known to most of you as Chubb's Tech . . .*

"It were the workhouse," Aunt Edith corrected, spraying crumbs.

PRESENTER: . . . *but now going up in the world.*

4. **Cut to large board screwed into wall, school front.** Board has white lettering on maroon base. At the center is name of school, times of opening, etc. Leaning up against it is a ladder. Camera follows Hard Man Sugden cautiously mounting a few rungs. He has a paint brush and a tin of paint. He begins to add gilt curlicues to a large name at bottom right-hand corner. This reads: CARETAKER, ERIC SUGDEN. Camera pans on to his back pocket, from which pokes a bottle of whiskey. It then

moves across the board to a much smaller name: PRINCIPAL, R. BEADLE. B.A. DIP. ED.

"Do you get the feeling that Rodney Beadle didn't do his homework on this program?" Bysshe asked.

"I tried to warn him, but he said that the only bad publicity is neglect. He's hooked on it."

5. **Move to school steps.** Presenter is walking up them, trailing a mike.

PRESENTER: *Going up in the world because the Principal, whose name you have just read, so I don't need to repeat it, has vision.*

6. **Cut to school entrance.** Camera moves to door of office, tries to fix on name which could be Principal but shot wavers and goes out of focus. Office door opens. Mr. Beadle comes out. Camera pulls back. Mr. Beadle hitches up trousers; scratches left buttock. He looks up, sees camera. Expresses momentary alarm. Then he comes to attention, pats his hair, shuffles feet to begin with left, and strides purposefully toward the camera. It retreats. Mr. Beadle quickens his pace. Still camera retreats, walls of corridor flying past. Mr. Beadle's smile becomes fixed. He begins to trot. As his figure grows smaller a hand is seen waving.

Noise over: Mr. Beadle, panting. **Cut.**

7. **Interior of school.** Day. Camera pans down stairs, along corridors. It pauses in the doorway of a classroom and rests on two students clamped in tight embrace. Camera sways, moves round room, rests on blackboard. Pause long enough for viewers to read: "Youth Training Scheme, 1. Some forms of nonverbal communication." **Fade out gradually.**

8. **Interior. Corridor.**

VOICE OF PRESENTER, OVER: *To the casual visitor Nathaniel Chubb might appear to be the standard model, the sort many of us are familiar with.*

9. **Camera enters cafeteria.** It lights upon bottles of tomato ketchup, moves to counter, follows a hand lining up plates of food. Baked beans slop over an edge; the hand scoops them back on to the plate.

"Noreen's on her usual form, anyway," Mog commented. "They didn't have to bribe her to do that."

PRESENTER'S VOICE, OVER: *But first impressions can deceive. In the words of the Principal, I quote . . .*

10. **Quick shot of Mr. Beadle's distant figure, waving.**

PRESENTER: *"Nathaniel Chubb is printing a whole new innovative expression upon the Changing Face of Education which frowns at no one, which offers courses tailored to all levels of aspiration and talent . . ."*

11. **Succession of fast shots:** Morris dancing; chocolate-Easter-egg making; indoor golf; car maintenance, with two pairs of legs, one male and one female, under partially dismantled car.

PRESENTER'S VOICE, OVER: *". . . and caters for all needs, whatever they may be."*

12. **Interior. Camera again sways down corridor.** It is approaching men's lavatory, as in take 2. It reaches the door, rests on name, bounces off, and finds women's lavatory opposite.

13. **Interior. Women's lavatory.** It is empty. Camera roves round, finds tampon dispenser, then moves to another. It is for male condoms. Camera rests on this for a few seconds, then **Fades.**

14. **Interior. Corridor.** Presenter stands with back to door of women's lavatory.

PRESENTER: *As a father said to me this morning, school's not like it was when I was a lad, and he couldn't have been more right. But did he mean better or worse? Stay with us and after the break* Taking the Lid Off *will be returning to Nathan-*

*iel Chubb to look more closely at the expression on Education's
Changing Face.*

"Wow!" Bysshe exclaimed.

"He's a fine example of the unregenerate male."

"The presenter? You're talking about the last shot? I'm not
so sure. Ged Taplow is clever. I reckon you could take your
choice between a laugh, censure or approval."

"Well, I hope Mr. Beadle is not influenced to change his
decision. I spent ages persuading him to install that."

"What was in that box on the wall in the lav?" Ben asked.

"Things men have to have now and again," Cyril answered.

"I know that!" Ben was scornful. "I meant the first box."

Bysshe was laughing. "You suggested it? I should have
guessed."

"Smelling salts," Great-aunt Edith pronounced loudly.

"Smelly salts? Why do they want them?"

"For when they have the vapors, Benjamin. Now, Grace, I'll
just take a cup of tea and a chicken-paste sandwich. I'm not
one for putting folks out."

"You'll rupture yourself if you go on like that much longer,"
Mog warned. "Blighted for life."

"Wouldn't want that, Doctor. Will take a rest on the bed.
You got it installed! Christ, Mog, you're brill."

"I don't know what you're talking about, Ben. My salt has
never gone smelly. I don't think it can. Here, carry this tray
into your auntie. And hurry; it's starting again."

Title rolls over still of exterior of the school. Music of brass
band playing the *Hallelujah Chorus,* slightly out of tune, over:

15. **Interior. School cafeteria.** It is half full. At a table in
the center sit the Presenter and Mr. Beadle. Mikes on booms
hover, ready to dive and snatch. Camera moves into the center, over Mr. Beadle's shoulder, and rests on Presenter's face.

PRESENTER: *As you say, Mr. Beadle, it is all a question of identifying a need.*

Camera draws back, locates the notice board on the wall beside the counter. It moves in and fixes on sheet of paper headed with name of Principal. This fills the screen. It is held long enough for viewers to read: There have been complaints from some individuals whose practice it is to stroll during clement weather along the path bordering the south elevation of the school. Though it is acknowledged that students on the upper stories may experience inconvenience caused by the distance to the toilets on the ground floor, it is necessary to insist on the immediate cessation of emergency measures as adumbrated above.

"Well, the mucky articles!" G. Aunt Edith gasped.

"A pity he forgot to remove that," Bysshe said. "No one knows what prompted it, anyway."

"I do."

"What's adumbrated?" Ben asked.

"You know as well as I do," Cyril rebuked. "And you've only got to let me catch you at it the once, and . . ."

"You'll have to save that piece of news till later, Mog. I'm still convalescing."

School cafeteria. Notice board. Gradually fades back to table.

PRESENTER: *In conversation with you, Mr. Beadle, I have noticed the importance you place on flexible planning. Can you tell our viewers something about that?*

MR. BEADLE: *Delighted.* (He swivels round, trying to face camera which remains behind him. Smiles graciously.) *But I think I should begin by making it clear to everyone that at our school nobody is ever turned away.* **Cut to:**

16. **Local comprehensive school. Mr. Dab's study.** He sits behind desk, smiling happily into camera.

MR. DAB: *As I was saying, I heard that Mr. Beadle had*

decided to close the German classes at the school since he could not justify the cost, so naturally I got in touch and offered to look after the disappointed students. It is working very well. I have a young master recently out of university who recognizes that it is in his interest to extend his experience, so a few additional lessons on his timetable are in the nature of a bonus rather than a task.

"He's slid out of it!" Mog shouted. "He's made Colin Banks, who teaches French, take it on! And I thought I'd settled him at last!"

"Don't tell me it was your suggestion, Mog, please. I shall displace an organ."

17. **School cafeteria as before.** Presenter and Mr. Beadle at table.

PRESENTER: *Perhaps you would like to take this opportunity to tell our viewers something about the courses at the school, Mr. Beadle.*

MR. BEADLE: *Delighted.* (Screws his head to face camera but his feet are in shot.) *In planning courses, I think I can claim without being accused of immodesty* (laughs) *that I am receptive to individual requirements. Sometimes a whole course has been devised around a single inquiry. Let me give you an example . . .*

Voice faded out as camera moves to Albert sitting alone at a table. He has a pile of newspapers in front of him. Opening one, he selects a photograph of a nude woman and with thick felt-tipped pen begins to cover her with yashmak, trousers, etc.

ALBERT: *Brazen hussy.*

Camera pulls away and returns to table with Presenter and Mr. Beadle. Mr. Beadle's voice faded in.

MR. BEADLE: *. . . should not like viewers to get the impression that we are all sombre and academic . . .*

PRESENTER: (Interrupting) *I am sure that is not the im-*

*pression they are getting, Mr. Beadle, not from where they are
sitting. But we must move on. You tell me that you see Chubb as
a community college that serves all interests and involves everyone in its schemes.*

MR. BEADLE: (Still trying to get head in frame) *I think I
should put that rather differently. We involve ourselves in everyone, not only in their work but in their play, in their total lives.
For example . . .*

PRESENTER: *I know you are about to tell us of the day
nursery, which you introduced for the first time this session, and
we shall be taking the viewers to see some of the kiddies later.*

MR. BEADLE: (Interrupting) *The day nursery represents a
totally new concept for the school. When I first had the idea I
saw it as a way of allowing women with babies to come into the
classes, but this soon developed into something very much more
experimental, not to say exciting . . .*

Voice faded out. Cut.

"It was my idea!" Mog raged. "He's taking all the credit!"

"Wait, Mog. They're doing some vicious editing. I should
not think Ged Taplow has finished with that one yet."

18. **School. Evening.** Groups of adults waiting to go into
evening classes. At a table sit Presenter and Mrs. Kitson.

"Oh, no!" Mog groaned.

PRESENTER: *We all have our ideas of excitement, and of
experiment, and if there are any men watching this program
tonight who would like to participate in one of the exciting ex-
periments that Mr. Beadle has thought up, then they can enroll
as baby minders in the day nursery.*

"He didn't think of it!"

PRESENTER: *And I, for one, would like to be a fly on the
wall when they tell their mates in the Fighting Cock.*

"I told you," Bysshe said.

"He's still in the Dark Ages."

"Yes; in television. Thinking of his ratings. He can't afford to antagonize half the population."

PRESENTER: *But for the ladies we can offer a different kind of excitement. Here on my right is Mrs. Kitson, and after the break she will be telling us about what she does at Nathaniel Chubb.*

Camera draws back. Cut to advertisements.

"He's the pits," Mog said. "I proposed the nursery. I got Walt and Pete to make the equipment. I got Pete on the rota. If it hadn't been for me it would never have happened and he's pretending it was entirely his idea. I feel like shoving his head through the screen."

"He'll be doing that himself by the end of the program, Mog. Haven't you noticed? They're taking the piss."

"I know, but the day nursery is something I promoted. It's important."

"Yes, and will remain so, whatever this crappy program makes of it."

"Without it, some of the women would not have been able to attend classes."

"Right. So you're laughing. Try, anyway. That's how it goes, Mog; the guy at the top picks up the honors. But don't worry. I think Rodney Beadle will regret it. Ged Taplow has got him on a hook, not because Beadle has lied, of course, but because it is Taplow's style. He's even made the introduction of men on the rota sound like a dirty joke."

"Caveman."

"You said our Maggie was going to be acting on this," Aunt Edith accused. "That's why I'm here, isn't it?"

"She'll probably be on after the break," Grace attempted to pacify.

"I haven't heard 'probably' before."

"I wanted to see them doing the dog training," Ben said. "I was hoping for a few hints."

"Now don't you let that Fred out before this is over," Aunt Edith ordered. "I want to die peaceful with all my five wits."

"Turn up the volume again, Cyril, please. It's coming back."

19. **Cafeteria. Evening.** Groups of adults moving out toward classrooms. Presenter at a table with Mrs. Kitson.

PRESENTER: *Here we are back with* Taking the Lid Off *at Nathaniel Chubb, where there has been an addition to the courses this session: an evening class in creative writing; and if Mrs. Kitson's experience is anything to go on, it has been highly successful. Tell me, Mrs. Kitson, when did you first realize that you had it in you to write a book?*

MRS. KITSON: (Smiling winsomely into the camera) *I suppose really when I was quite a tiny tot.*

PRESENTER: *And why was that?*

MRS. KITSON: (Slightly thrown) *Well, I . . . er . . . I . . . was always jotting down something. Stories. My teacher used to say that I had a way with words.*

PRESENTER: *And she was certainly right, Mrs. Kitson. You've got a way with words. Would you be kind enough to read some to our viewers?*

MRS. KITSON: (Radiant) *Well, I do think it is spiffing of you to . . .*

PRESENTER: *Tell us what the book is called, Mrs. Kitson.*

MRS. KITSON: *The title is* Hot Days, *but I do not want you to think it is not respectable, you see . . .*

PRESENTER: *Now don't spoil our viewers' enjoyment, Mrs. Kitson. You've got them perched on the edge of their seats. So now, viewers, prepare yourselves for a rendering from* Hot Days, *which will be out on the shelves next spring.*

"She's got it accepted, Bysshe! And I gave her the plot! Any minute now I shall go bananas."

MRS. KITSON: *You want me to start? Well, here goes.* "*The party was going full swing. Out in the garden, lanterns of oriental design hung in the bushes and lit the imaginative costumes of the guests as they stepped to the rhythm of a romantic waltz.*" *I haven't explained that it is a fancy-dress party. You see* (Catches the Presenter's eye), *oh dear, I'm interrupting myself, aren't I? Sorry.* "*Crystal stood alone by the French windows that led into the huge drawing room of Mr. Dupont's private mansion. Miserably her eyes followed a handsome cavalier in curly wig and velvet cloak, the magnificent disguise Mr. Dupont had chosen. She was sure he had recognized her in her pretty milkmaid gown, but he had not asked her to dance. Instead, he was giving all his attention to a young woman dressed as Nell Gwyn. Watching, Crystal felt the hot tears roll down her cheeks.*"

"Mog, stop grinding your teeth."

"I don't want to listen to any more."

"I was just beginning to lose myself in it."

"It's not funny."

"Hastily he bit back the tactless reminder that she, too, had once written such a book."

"No, I haven't. At least, only as far as chapter four. It got changed."

MRS. KITSON: "*Then she felt an arm around her waist. Crystal started. 'At your service, Lovely. Would you honor me with this dance?' There was no need for her to turn to check who was by her side and for a moment her heart leapt with sympathy for Desmond Leeming, whose patient, loyal and undemanding love over so many years she had been unable to requite. Then she saw Mr. Dupont draw Nell Gwyn aside and whisper to her. Crystal's mood suddenly changed. She would show him! She*

*would make him suffer as he did her! Quickly she turned to
Desmond. 'Yes,' she breathed. 'Let us dance.' Essaying a laugh,
she drew him on to the lawn. Eagerly Desmond took her in his
arms. She could feel the fervor of his heart beat through his
sequined coat, and she made no movement of refusal when in
the middle of the dance he stopped and, embracing her passion-
ately, kissed her full on the mouth. As he did so, over his shoulder she saw Mr. Dupont. His eyes had not missed a trick and
were startled, disbelieving, and wide with a passion that could
only be described as jealousy. Crystal smiled to herself as Desmond resumed the dance."*

"Oh, no!"

"I bet Les D'Arcy freaked out after that paragraph, Mog."

"I couldn't do that. I simply couldn't do it! It's odd, I never
anticipated there would be anything you could not bring yourself to write."

"Or do."

"Oh, Bysshe!"

PRESENTER: *I'm afraid that is all the time I can allow you,
Mrs. Kitson. We don't want to spoil the plot for your readers.*

"I don't think much to that," Cyril remarked. "Our Maggie
could knock that into a cocked hat any day of the week."

PRESENTER: *I am sure all our viewers will join me in wishing you the best of luck with* Hot Days, *Mrs. Kitson, but before
you go I suspect that they would like me to ask you a question.
Has Mr. Kitson read* Hot Days *yet?*

MRS. KITSON: *Oh, no. I wouldn't dream of bothering him.
He prefers watching the television.*

PRESENTER: *Sound man. So, viewers, you have had a taste
of the first fruits of Nathaniel Chubb's writing class . . .*

"Nan Glen will be furious."

"I should think her back is broad enough."

PRESENTER: *And it is nearly time to go. Tonight* Taking the Lid Off *has been looking at Chubb and examining the ideas of its Principal, whose vision is to make this old foundation which was once a no-nonsense technical school, into a community college that serves the needs of everyone in the town.*

Fade out and immediately fade into:

20. **Corridor outside room in which day nursery is housed.** Presenter by door.

PRESENTER: (Into camera) *So, if the ladies want to read Mrs. Kitson's* Hot Days *they can send their husbands to mind the babies in the day nursery. And that is where we end, with the toddlers who may one day form Mr. Beadle's student population, learning right from the start that Chubb's is not all somber and academic.*

21. **Interior. Classroom housing nursery.** Presenter in center. The room is decked out for a Christmas party: tree, somewhat bedraggled, streamers, a trestle covered with the debris of party food, spilled orange juice. The children look hot, tired, and fractious; they are being lined up by the anxious mothers to receive their presents.

PRESENTER: (Into mike, whispering portentously) *I don't want to give away any trade secrets, but in case you don't recognize Father Christmas we will just remind you of what he looks like in less formal gear.*

Cut to:

22. **Rerun of take of Mr. Beadle running down the corridor toward the camera.** It has been quickened up. Mr. Beadle is seen to sweat profusely. **Cut.**

23. **Return to nursery.** Children's party. Mr. Beadle is sitting on a chair in one corner. A boom hangs over his head. He looks up at it apprehensively. He is dressed in traditional

robes, heavily whiskered, but part of the beard is loose. He keeps trying to stick it back. He reaches down for the thin boy who starts to cry. Trying to control the boy's struggles and hold beard at same time, he is flustered. He raises his head and speaks directly into the mike.

MR. BEADLE: (Sound amplified) *One of them pulled it off when I was kissing her.*

PRESENTER: (Into his mike, camera on him, winking) *Could have been worse! Sorry, ladies.*

"I bet that was Suzy."

"No; she's next."

"Crikey! I didn't recognize her in that dress. Poor kid."

Camera on Mr. Beadle. The sound is very low so that his mouth is seen moving but no words are heard. He is attempting to find out the thin boy's name but receives only answering yells. Eventually he gives up, digs in his bag, fishes out a parcel, hands it to the thin boy who drops it, and swings him unceremoniously off his knee. Mr. Beadle looks up and realizes that the camera is on him. He draws a hand across his forehead and attempts to smile. The whiskers drip. He bends over Suzy.

MR. BEADLE: *Come along, little girl.* (Lifts her onto his knee. She does not resist but when on, squirms and looks about her.) *And what's your name?* (Sound coming up)

SUZY: (She glares into the camera, looking as if she is going to spit) *Suzy.*

24. **Camera draws back. Credits roll across screen.** Title: *Taking the Lid Off*

Voice over: *The program that brings you facts without tears.*

25. **Mix. Nursery in background. Presenter in foreground.**

PRESENTER: *See you next week, folks.* (Pretends to turn away, then looks back) *Oh, and let me remind you: if you want*

*anything a bit special, you can be sure of finding it at Nathaniel
Chubb. Or can you?*
Cut to:
Mr. Beadle with Suzy on his knee.
MR. BEADLE: *And what do you want Father Christmas to
bring you for Christmas, Suzy?*
SUZY: (Sound very high. Suzy takes huge breath) *A penis.*
Camera on Mr. Beadle. He recoils. His hands drop from
Suzy's waist. He gasps, drawing in whiskers. As he begins to
cough, **Cut.**

"I don't know why we are laughing," Mog said at last.

"I do."

"As far as I am concerned, Suzy's wanting a penis for
Christmas is subversive."

"Mog, she's only four!"

"Obviously Action Man was a big mistake."

"It would have made no difference had he been more con-
ventionally endowed."

"I wish you'd stop rolling about. It's not comic."

"Not realistic. And I like it. But I can appreciate why Rodney Beadle was less enthusiastic. Poor chap. The way Ged
Taplow took him apart was unfair."

"It wasn't! He deserved it. He's a pseud."

"He's that all right but, as he said, receptive to individual
requirements. He installed that dispenser in your loos, Mog. I
haven't recovered from that yet. And he agreed to start the
nursery. You have to give him credit for that, whatever his
motives."

"I suppose so."

"No supposing. It's a fact, and will stay. You've made a
valuable point."

"But not with Mrs. Kitson."

"Win some; lose some."

"I can't see that I have won any."

There was Suzy wanting a penis; and Mrs. Kitson placing *Hot Days,* which was based on her plot; and Nan Glen submitting Keith's poems to a magazine; and Mrs. D'Arcy rejecting *An Anatomy of Passion;* and Keith turned on by Mike's book and telling Josephine that the first experiment had been unsatisfactory; and Josephine drooling over the prospect of more serious application; and Mr. Beadle pretending that he had thought of the day nursery; and Mr. Dab wriggling out of the job she had planned for him, once again winning hands down.

"I've lost all down the line," she said, wearied and mournful.

"I'd like to think not. Feel like having another go?"

"How do you mean?"

"He lay back on his narrow bed and considered her face. The strong bones were highlighted by the glare from the unshaded lamp, for he was an unemployed lodger in a small terrace bed-sit and could not afford the luxury of the soft lighting that he knew was routine for the moment that, for many weeks now—how many he could not calculate—had troubled yet excited him in his dreams. Her expression changed as he spoke. Was she, he asked himself, getting his gist? But that was perhaps too much to hope. She was capable of unbelievable obtuseness; in times past she had ignored little hints he had timorously made to her, partly because she had once taken a vow against his sex. Now, despite her assurance that she had reversed that, he feared that some of her prejudice might linger. For she was a woman of action and he merely an observer of man's eternal quiddities. 'Margaret,' he uttered painfully, 'there is something between us that has to be said.' Your turn, Mog."

"And she looked down at her hands folded in her lap. His words had confused her. During the last three months she had struggled with the conundrums of emotions, with contradictory sensations, with the investigation of profundities . . ."

"I like that."

"Shut up! And what had it brought her? Dross. The lees of passion, the bitterness of remorse. For she knew she had behaved insensitively. She had taken this man's attention and sympathy for granted . . ."

"You don't have to say that, Mog. It's in your letter."

". . . while she had gone her own way, trying to find answers, but with no success."

"Hang on. My turn again. But one answer she could be certain of, if she would only listen. It was that he loved her energy, her individuality, her blinkered obsessions . . ."

"Please be frank."

"Of course. Look, I can't provide uncritical infatuation."

"Do I get obsessed with things?" Like her father.

"Just a bit." He grinned. "But you are interrupting the flow. Where was I? Oh, yes. He loved her blinkered obsessions, which revealed an endearing talent for getting herself in a mess. There you are; you can smile again. And, too, her independence, most of all that. Surely she knew by now that their thoughts played the same track; that theirs would be a relationship based on equality; that she would never have to strive to make him understand; that he, like her, was a democrat? Christ, Mog, this is growing heavy."

Her mouth was dry. It was years since she had eaten. Perhaps all she needed was a cup of tea, then her legs would be less rubbery.

"We ought to try writing one together," she said.

"You mean, you supply the plots and I take care of the fancy bits?"

She laughed, remembering Denis's proposal at the first writing class. Then she recalled "eternally in my voluptuous thoughts." "It's strange, but I thought of that once myself, with the fancy bits done by someone else."

"I can believe you."

"He wouldn't have written them so well."

"You think not? Why?"

"Not realistic enough. At the time."

"Ah. But that is not a requirement."

"For me, it is."

"I had guessed that."

There was a pause.

"Like a cup of tea?" Bysshe asked.

"It was not that sort of realism I was thinking of."

"Me neither." He got up and stood by her chair. "You know, I think we can improve on Cupid Books."

And they did.

About the Author

JUNE OLDHAM was raised in a small village in Lincolnshire, in England. A graduate of the University of Manchester, she received a Bachelor of Arts degree in English Language and Literature and taught English for several years.

Ms. Oldham now writes full time and has written several children's books as well as an award-winning adult novel. She recently directed the Ilkley Literature Festival and teaches creative writing part time.

Ms. Oldham is married and lives with her actor husband and two children in West Yorkshire, where the author enjoys walking on the moors not far from her home.

Grow Up, Cupid is Ms. Oldham's first book for Delacorte Press.